Modern Confessions

Gopal Chowdhary

First published in 2020 by

BecomeShakespeare.com

One Point Six Technologies Pvt. Ltd.
119-123, 1st floor, Building No. J2, Wadala East,
Wadala Truck Terminal, Mumbai, Maharashtra 400037, India
T: +91 8080226699

ISBN: 978-93-90266-70-8

DEDICATED TO

The fiction is dedicated to all those characters, events and eventualities, actions and their results in the fiction. But for them, it would not have been possible to conceive this novel. It was these characters and events that would make me to write this. They would come like doves and would dovetail and spin their stories. The Novelist would be just the ground for grounding of their being and doings!

DISCLAIMERS

All events and characters in this fiction are fictitious and imaginary. Any resemblance is incidental and for that author or publisher is not responsible.

ACKNOWLEDGEMENTS

The writer acknowledges the contribution of existence and existents in making happen this work.

PREFACE

One night a man sees a dream. In the dream, he has become flower. A flower that blossoms and lives just for being flower. He wants to be just flower adding beauty to the garden that life is. When he wakes up, he is in doldrums: the dream that he saw was real or the real life was dream. He could not decide which the real was and which dream.

Since then he believes that he is a flower seeing the dream of being man. And that dream he continues.

On the other side of world, a woman believes that she is a bird seeing the dream of being woman. She goes to an indeterminate space and time. Before that, there was no space and time. She was the bird and whole skies her nest. She happened to meet a man dreaming about being bird! Both were real and unreal at the same time. They would start living in a space that is dreaming to be time and the time dreaming to be space.

One day they have doubt as to who they are? What is real and what is dream. They are the real or the dream that sees is real. They decide to go to a teacher or guru. When they ask the teacher, he says that he is having same problem. The teacher has seen a dream that he is neither man nor woman but just a being who is dreaming that he or she is life itself. And he continues to live in that dream.

They also decide to keep on living like what they are! Real and dream are ephemeral! But the life is real and dreams both.

FOREWORD

Every age, times, generation, and space think they are the modern. They are the best, the human history and the life on earth has epitomized into them, their generations, time and age. The breakthrough achievements, cultural and civilization heights are they themselves. There is 'end of freedom', after and before they are the best. Then next and next; it goes on and on.

It is not like that they are boasting, it is perhaps because life is process and it goes on and on, in one form or another. Here or there. Everywhere and nowhere! Everything or nothing, its same in one or other way. From nothing everything comes from and goes into nothing, and then goes into new life and existence! Its existence, life and its playfield is world. All have been competing with their respective truths until other proves it irrelevant if not wrong.

For the life and its truth churning has not stopped yet. It keeps on churning till infinity with our karmas and actions n its result, cause and effect. And dynamics of karmas are matchless and infinite. *Udho! Karman ki gati Nyari!*

ABOUT THE AUTHOR

The Author has written few academic books and one Hindi Novel, Wo to Nahi. It is his debut English novel.

PROLOGUE

I live, because I think so. If I do not think I do exist. If I think, existence becomes non-existent sort of things! But I continue to live and tick for existence! As of now I have ceased to think therefore I do exist. But I certainly exist beyond thinking and thought: in flesh and muscles. In body, breast and thighs and center! So we have stopped thinking just to exist: In the multiplicity of beings, thoughts, and the scenes, fast changing, with fast cut.

Am I a being? Or non-being with too many beings crowding and choking the being. The multiplicity of beings: This, that and everything. All types of experimentation. Bi, Straight, hetero, acting like tv and msg? What is truth: money, ambition, flesh, body or chasing the dreams after dreams? Or not believing in any truth. That is my truth. Because there is not one truth, but the multiple ones: multiple truths of multitude!

Split personality or split beings or multiplicity of beings! Null, void and confusion, nausea! Loneliness! Reeking into multiplicity and multiple partners, Individuality of sexuality and the sexuality of the individuality. Denying truth, universal laws and percepts are the new mantra of life! Resurrecting no self or fluid one if any, out of this cancelation of self!

Homes within home-hierarchal and lateral both in dimension and diametrically opposed to each other as well. Parallelism of unparalleled! Without walls, and the inhabitants co-opted with virtual selves and family space. No kids till 40s! The best if no kid at all! The other modern culture is flooding the earth with their respective sons and daughters of gods, to make whole world theirs.

This is typical of us moderns! We say no kids, while others are child producing machine, out to make world crowded with respective dominations! We preach peace, non-violence, freedom and democracy, and we are more violent, freedom has become a sort of fetter! While democracy is gasping for breath on many fronts, we are going gaga over it.

The wars, genocide and mayhem by the moderns have been unprecedented in scale, number, intensity and brutality. Even tribal record would pale before ours! Since we are modern, does it more in all respects. The tribalization of modern and the modernization of tribal ethos and credos! But the test tube baby, IV and surrogacy are also there. Despite the fact that Kids are considered hindrance to free and unbound enjoyment of life.

Here, in our modern homes, we do not seem to be living. We just come to rest and sleep probably. Our respective homes have shifted to diverse one: Virtual corner, multiplicity of personalities, beings, life styles, no hold barred hangouts, and outdoor life! Our shadows live. They become active at day, we at night.

When Sun is up, we drop dead like shadow or invisible, metaphorically and literally as well. Knowledge has been cancelled, soul has been denied, and consciousness and inner self has been denied. On that debris existential and otherwise hollow freedom, multiplicity and pluralism has been built like house of cards amidst shifting sands. Though these are visible to the self yet remains invisible to world. We like darkness—desire, dream, to reek and chill in all and with all without any restriction. No ifs and buts, no good or bad carping, morality and social norms blabalaa.

Sun-knowledge, soul are anathema to us. They force us to be within boundary, to warn and guide, they say, but is sort of interference to us, it is best that our immediate successor-postmodernists have canceled, what is said in Hindi: if no bamboo tree, there will be no flute! The voice of inner self, the consciousness seems to have been lost in infinite space of thoughts, desires and cravings. This is the life that is also the life.

Everything and everyone is the life. Live them!

 No bad no good things exist in reality. They are what they are: we tag them with good or bad. So it is better to have no judgment, and not being judgmental or soul searching. Keep on going without any hangover, pangs of pain and repentance comes and goes out. What matters only pleasure, a good and free life at our whims and fancies all that counts! We could extract pleasure even from pain like woman getting pleasure from pain!

CONTENTS

PART
1

1

CONFESSION OF AN UNKNOWN MODERN

Hi! I'm modern. Actually postmodern or post-postmodern! Whatever way you see I am there. We do not believe in any belief. So do I, not believing in any belief, even if be it my belief! For us, the world and the society and its norms are a sort of restriction. Restricts our freedom, yours and mine to be free.

I exist, because I think so. If I do not think I do exist. If I think, existence becomes non-existent sort of things! But I continue to live and tick for existence! As of now I have ceased to think therefore I do exist. But I certainly exist beyond thinking and thought: in flesh and muscles. In body, breast and thighs and center! So we have stopped thinking just to exist: In the multiplicity of beings, thoughts, and the scenes, fast changing, with fast cut.

Am I being? Or non-being with too many beings crowding and muffling the being. The multiplicity of beings: This, that and everything. All types of experimentation. Bi, Straight, hetero, acting like tv and msg? What is truth: money, ambition, flesh, body or chasing the dreams. Or not believing in any truth. That is my truth. Because there is not one truth, but the multiple ones: multiple truths of multitude!

Split personality or split beings or multiplicity of beings! Null, void and confusion, nausea! Loneliness! Reeking into multiplicity and multiple partners, Individuality of sexuality and the sexuality of the individuality. Denying truth, universal laws and percepts are the new mantra of life! Resurrecting no self or fluid one if any, out of this cancelation of self!

Negation of God and in that place creating new gods of consumerism, crass materialism, technology, rituals, myopic dream of Swarg (Heaven), non existing kingdom of god, negation of everything. Then it becoming playground of multiple lives, individualities, personality, way of life culture bordering on tribalism, promiscuousness unbound and legalized.

Sex—one of the natural and basic instincts out of many is all! Eyes are because voyeurism is there. Face is there because narcissism is there. Thirst and hunger is because consumerism is there. Gratifications all that seems to be mattering to the moderns and their successive generations. It has got the exaltation of individuality, and the sexuality has acquired a status and important component of one's personality and freedom.

And the sexuality appears to have become a fashion and a sort of fad. Not overtly in all cases and incidents but covertly for sure, it has been uplifted to the sublime of love, right and natural justice. Like many I partly subscribe: sex part and love. It is life and here you get love, happiness. No Respite from millions of desires, zillions of thoughts and fantasies. I want to live all those. This is what life is, what they say.

My friend, Anu has been searching her being. She seeks her freedom in changing partner every other night. That is her life, and she has every right to do so. But the being that is searching the real being is that the being we are hankering after! What is it? A different being or the same being! She has not found her ideal partner, because there is no ideal only mundane appearing ideal.

I hope not confusing or sounding like so. Everything is true except the truth. The Truth has been cancelled. Everybody has to find his or her truth. It is not necessary that my truth coincides or not with all truths and facts. It should be right and truth in my way. Back to logical illogicality!

Freedom is gratification of desires, beings, and natural instincts. Consume, use and throw and use things as doormat etcetera .Only the convenience and the priority of mine over others that matters to us. And do what titillates us. Gratification of senses, flesh, ambition, and dark desires n taboo. Even incest is not unwelcome on condition of titillation and gratification, of course not known to the world.

Nothing is sacrosanct. If it could be enjoyed; enjoy, without getting caught. It is not cheating or thieving till caught, do the thieving but do not get caught. This is not what I say, it is what system gives impression: percept and norms. Though not in theory yet certainly in practice, in praxis, to speak academically. Anything that hinders us, restricts us is non freedom.

Or cheating with tacit and tactical consent! Cheating without getting caught is not cheating for us moderns and postmodern and all! Exploring the life in the multiplicity, reeking freedom in sex, love and backstabbing! Even if caught, it's worth getting caught. Swinging and swapping. With or without consent, steal extra love, sex; and illicit and discreet relations going on. If not explored, it's your loss.

The moderns and post moderns appear to have been living in crisis. And in dealing with one crisis they have been creating another crisis and to solve that giving rise to another, and on and on. Crisis after crisis…... Even if there is no crisis, they would create, invent, feign and manufacture crisis. Why! It seems to be rather logical fallacy of illogical thinking, just for sympathy, satisfaction to their plummeting self esteem, votes and elections, score over one other community, culture, religion, caste, color, creed. Language, gender and class like enclosures.

The same enclosures and division of primitive! Stark us vs them as if to finish each other if possible, mutual hostility and hatred masked under the civility of words, narrative, and percepts. The difference of creed, class, color, caste, blood and kinship, honor and the filial bondage seem to be tribal redo of modernity!

Only religion, culture, class and ideology have been added form point zero of tribalism to the height of modernity! And that too seems to have become other enclosures! The outer covers might be wrapped in the modern diction and jargons but inside seems to be but betraying the primeval traits at worst and pre-modern one at the best.

The Nature never plays dice. But the moderns have been playing dangerous game of dice with Nature. The modern humans have not left any natural things, natural laws, natural entities and elements like earth, sky, ether, water, earth from its greed. The euphoric mastery over them, win over the nature by science and technology, reckless exploitation, plunder, and the loot. Rape of nature has been happening to prove the greed, ego and mastery of humans over nature. The tribal mindset of loot and plunder!

Moderns inter personal and intra personal, their community and inter and intra community, their society and inter and intra societal relations, their nations and inter and intra nations relation, all are characterized by this domineering and exploitative relations, undercut by simmering us vs. them, mutual bickering and urge to dominate and comeuppances, out to prove other inferior. And they have very smartly and cunningly wrapped them with various modern epithets, jargon and diction such as freedom, liberty, democracy and equality of unequal!

If it is so, be what anybody could do. If these are the ugly under belly of the modernity, we have to live it. There is no other option available: leave it or take it. Why leave it, why not take it, try to be as it has to be, make it best and enjoy it.

But age is catching on. Life is losing its virility. Suck the juices of life. Mount of Venice. Not sermon on mounts. End of freedom and end of everything. There is nothing to achieve as everything has been through and nowhere to go as space, time, knowledge, God, and the Life, existence has been denied.

What matters are the matter, form, and body! Consume and gratify! Do everything that gives individuality, a feeling to be master of fleeting things; master having mastery over no holds barred pleasure and more pleasure. My life man! My world! My body. Vagina speaks! Penis thunders! That is where all discourse ends after starting from it!

It does not matter that we have no control over our own birth and death. Even if we do not have control over 90 per cent of our body! So what! Mastery over the use or misuse of nature, nurture, sex, freedom and right are worth trying. If it is happening at macro level of system or existence, it is bound to trickle down to micro. While at one level it is wrong, other level it is not so. It means there is no good or bad, it is matter of perception and convenience too.

For us, there is no other. Other is not hell but heaven! To enjoy with, to love and make love! It is they who give me real being. My life ticks through them. Life realizes through them! How could be they 'other'? They are extension of me or you honey!

Life is ticking. Age is catching on, time slipping. Grab what we can: in war n love everything is fair. Love has shifted to the flesh and flesh to the love. Centre becoming periphery making it centre (of attraction) centric. Form, body, flesh, and the multiplicity that is what seems to be sum total of life. No boundary has remained. All boundaries and limitations have tumbled down. If they stumble upon, do they certainly, accept as it were not there. With love, happiness, freeing of ego and dissolving it in all that unfold before us.

That is what post- postmodernism is! Perhaps! Don't know, not sure either. Even they are not sure about postmodernism and post-postmodernism! How could we the lesser mortals!

But it is good and a sort of banal boon for us modernist also. Enjoy, consume, and fornicate, promiscuousness sanctioned indirectly, homosexuality and lesbian legalized. No hold barred. Did wrong! No problem repent, face the music of law. Reform or perish. But keep on enjoying that unbound and no hold barred that has been accepted, in disguised way if not in indirect way, as life, freedom and individuality!

2
MAAN AND KAJAL

One day we- my live in partner, Kajal-felt bored of everything! Even the sex and love had become routine and boring, a sort of mechanical activities. She with high sex drive but posing as low and I with outright high drive! We both were hankering after heterotypic! She was blaming me and I her. Not married formally we were at large for everything. Every possibility can be explored, at the same having the advantage of not being tied to any anything or person.

My father and mother were very upset with me. We had not settled and got married to have child. But these settled things would unsettle me: it would rattle the whole being and personality. The very idea of being tied to a person, place and relationship had been unnerving from childhood. It seemed to me as a sort of bondage, restricting the freedom to be and doing what one likes when free! My parents were farmer with straight and simple bent of mind. They could not understand me, and their simple and straight life in village could not appeal to me. That is why I shifted to a metropolitan city from primary school days. Others of my siblings remained stay put there!

My farmer father came to know, through some village gossip mouth, about my live in partner, Kajal. He would become very disheartened. What he would say to the traditional village folks and how would he explain it to them. This question had disturbed him more than anything else. He had no hope from me ever since I left village life for the glitter and the fast life of the metropolitan city. He had only warned me: Maan you are playing with fire!

Maan, that's my name and my live in partner, is Kajal. The other day we were sitting in garden, trying to pep up our sagging life. We were role playing of a kid. It was just to pep up the failing excitement in the life, and the colors in life instead flying were floundering colorless. We were in for some dirty things. Then I noticed one guy in 20s hidden across the bush of park tomfooling. With his in hand and perhaps self jerks. I got excitement. I noticed the partner also eyeing, and we got excited. The passion and love seemed to have returned.

But the guy was gazing at us, rather in the transfixed way. Brazenly and rudely but she was loving it. Had I not been or permitted she would have swallowed him there.

'Hi! u r great! She was praising and encouraging him and I liked her! We could be friend in deed indeed!

'I don't have home. I am new to here, the guy was saying

'I will guide you, she had fallen for him. Me too for 3s and bi things perhaps!

Scene would shift to the car. Mid way to the hilly resort! And driving SUV. In car mirror they were being seen cuddling to each other....she took him in his hand. Mirror does not speak lies. Oh god! she had taken all! I felt also excitement, as if along with her I also woman. My right hand also touched his, measuring his in her. As if it was signal; they for marathon, young and young. Car would be jerking in back seat.

We would be slowing down the speed. Then stopping to a

lonely stretch, started enjoying rather bizarre excitement. She was busy with the guy. I : spectator. A spectator would be beholding and seeing the mirror. Both were into each other. I would also get into it. Three or it would seem one; in love he would become mine and she was already mine. So where would be other, he would be mine and she is already mine. All would be one and one the all!

But it would be wrong…morally and legally. Against the law of land! Space and time constraints! They say, but he or she, I and she would be one and there would be no other. Who would pass judgment we were wrong. The judgment has been postponed at the worst. At the best, judgment is in process to be delivered indefinitely as knowledge, conscience and soul have been cancelled. Who could pass the judgment when subject and object have become one and the ground shifting like the shifting sands!

For outer world it might be wrong but our inside would not be seeing it as such. Since outside is the extension and the projection of the inside, how could be it wrong! Even if It might be wrong morally and legally. This is logical advantage of modernity: one could prove right as wrong and wrong as right. Even if it is logical fallacy!

There was one more redeeming ground! We had not been caught by any one. A thief is not thief unless caught. And neither any of us would have intention to reveal our pleasure and individuality dark horse to anyone. Nor To Outside world! And Conscience has already been pronounced a dead wood! To our advantage!

Knock…. Knock. On front window of our car!

Knock… knock knocking, in the rear where we three were being one: he in her and I was already in her.

A Policeman would be knocking at the car door: Highway patrol. But it was going to be freeway leisure trip. On the window pane he would get stuck like glue. Trying to become one: With prospect of 3 becoming 4 one. We had broken law. He amended it by kissing and piling on all over her. Uprooting us; first he would do from she and then me.

Cut to custody! Group and bondage and 4 s! He ordered: get in proper dress. And trying to hold her hand to take her to the secluded place.

'The dress, you call proper or improper, you brute, she would yell You just bite me all over. You do these things to your mother…

'You would be handcuffed, you slut, the policeman warned. You are slutting around n trying to be Sati Savitri. You sexy slut! He cooed down, we winked.

'She is my wife, not slut! Mind your language, I said with no confidence of husband as I was not. He pushed me back in car. He caught hold her hand, staggering her towards the secluded place. We pounced upon him but he overpowered us. And locked us in car tying our feet with rope!

After wriggling out our self from the policeman rope, we ran frantically towards where he had disappeared with her in jungle. A jungle out there! With all its eerie silence, mysterious and thrilling aura, it would appear as dark belly of nature. Hardly 100 meters down in the jungle, had we gone. We would stop after listening to the two people conversing in friendly way.

'We are from decent family, It was Kajal, with high profile job. We gave lift to him and it accidently happened. I lost control or swept off by passion. Hubby was just mediating the entanglement!

When you came in…..

It was my live-in partner voice--crisp, husky and sexy when in good mood. But there was silence. Something happening between them… we got suspicious.

'I understand, the policeman was heard chuckling:… but you will have to be our guest tonight as part of punishment.

We heard him laughing and she also joining rather cuttingly.

'Well… well I have to consider, now it was her turn … in fact ask hubby for it.

I felt relieved of the phantom tension building inside. Its right time to make our entry, whispered our sexy guy. The guy was more than happy after seeing her from forced separation.

'Come …come welcome, the policeman was cooing. Then roared rather jokingly, the judgment has been passed. The punishment has been pronounced. You all will have to be my guest tonight at nearby farmhouse.

'Did he say tonight or today, asked the sexy guy. I just ignored. He would sound irritated as he was suffering from the pang of separation from her.

1

We were returning from the policeman farm house. The car was moving amidst the lush green hill tops and valleys of Aravalis. It was just not a party hosted in our honor. It was a gangbang. The live-in partner was really acting like slut. Did not know there existing a slut in her. I eyed her sitting in front seat of car, beside me.

I was at driving wheel and the guy was sleeping on the rear seat. She was playing sex game. In between she would be browsing adult site and real time action slots! That too in aftermath of performing marathon, and she would be as fresh as the morning dew on flowers. We were going to our pre-booked resort. To enjoy and drown ourselves in no hold barred freedom.

Gang bang of the policeman party! Real-time, and off time! One in all! Still craving for more! And my cravings growing too in proportion to her heightening frenzy. In between she would not forget to poke the sleeping guy, touching mine as well his. She is really slut. Is she mine or the same guy I courted? She is different still mine. Our love and marriage (of live-in partnership) love seemed to have got fresh lease, thinking I started whistling!

I kissed her and she responded passionately. And lo and behold soon we would be making passionate and violent love on front seat of car. In that wilderness on way to hilly resorts we were going to. Earth had started shaking. Sky was already reeling overhead. And then our sexy guy would wake up.

Initially in his drowsiness he would think we were fighting. But when he saw our passionate fight a romantic duel, he joined the front car bonanza from the rear. Metered by her groping of him! No fear of law. As law had become friend. We were the law. There would be no other: person, society and world. We were the world, we would be the law to our self, and all that would matter.

Where is other! It is just extension of self—myself, herself, his self, policeman self and every one. Sky, Sun, moon, river, mountain, jungle—appearing one, as extension of the self! Sex and desire like wine seem to be transcending all barriers just to satiate and fulfill it.

We would reach the holiday resort in the evening. A beautiful resort indeed! Surrounding lush green mountains overlooked by the parrot green valley, and a rivulet flowing down the stream. We checked in, well that what they say honeymoon suit. With side and even overhead roof was 3Dmirror walled. Seeing guy and wife cuddling, kissing and surreptitiously fondling each other like newly married. The resort allotted honeymoon suit with some heckles drawn. The presence of third—me or him— had raised their heckles initially. But I soothed their feathers: nephew of mine! The guy was a bit nut. Mental sort of things! Always wanting to be with uncle and aunties, I would say.

But not sure whether it would raise more heckles. Never minding we checked in. What a suite! Walled glass with 3d effect . I was Wonder struck, and the guy moonstruck, pouncing upon each other like hungry cats. I just got stuck up in the scene. Bewildered and lost: and feeling how she might be feeling. It would be giving immeasurable excitement and passion like that of woman!

The guy was doing my work; first ramming his tongue into hers. Peeling of the skinny and skimpy brazier less top! The round shaped baby melon shaped breast he was sucking. And I was watching. I would be getting excitement not out of mine but what she was enjoying as woman. She would look towards me before taking the sugar candy, as if for approval. And she got it and they were like the long lost lovers.

Thinking to give them space, I sauntered towards ante room. It was a bit dark there. They could not see me but I could. Bed with sofa was there. I would be resting and watching them play the game of love. No sooner than they were into pre-fore play stage I was glued. She was guiding him.. Here feeling like 6s, thanks to the 3 D wall and roof mirror. Apparent and real would be getting mixed to the utter confusing pleasure!

And everything had got dissolved in that effect: all boundaries, limitations. Morality and blabalaa that would be considered hindrance but proving to be booster doze of love making! But it was surreal, rather bizarre or didn't know what! She with him! Both naked and game of love would be going in full swing. The seer would be becoming the scene!

With everywhere, all over room, it was their bodies entangling. Clasped! Some time moving, shaking most of the time! And I was just being viewer and would be getting titillation as if I were her! My love, my partner and the guy not rival but young, rude and passionate lover and beloved both!

The 3d effect of her bust, his mouth on her and clasped body. Oh it was embarrassing and at the same time exciting as well. Was I getting stuck by voyeurism? Getting the gratification from watching her moon struck with him! Now she would be cooing and moaning. She was more like Mountain River threatening to submerge him. I had started doing and feeling what she was undergoing: cooing and moaning, as if had been penetrated by him, not she getting that! Now fingering as he would enter her as if he had entered me and lo and behold, clouds were thundering with passion!

When through, both were lying like dead weight of soft and light passion, juice-soaked and partaking it too. She withdrew from him, juices of both passions overflowing slowly and steadily. Then I would be doing to him like she had done to him. Moaning and gasping. Come baby come baby. She had started protesting as if stealing her lover! He was her treasure trove. Her lover and now being stolen!

Cat and fog fought had started. She had turned slut nay she was a slut and a sort of whoring whore, I could not but help from thinking. That was why so much possessive about police man she was that day. A whore fighting for her hunt being whored, I concluded rather witchingly!

Pack up. Shooting stopped. Back to home! We left the orphaned guy at hotel. All payment made. Additional money for guy! To go home and few more money for whoring him, he was so much exhausted from love! He seemed to have dropped dead, she said.

2

Home! That great civilization home seems to have withered away. Only house has remained with all four walls and roof! Great home has lost to shadow homes or virtual homes. Or homes within home! Virtual homes of every family member: social media, net, sites, whatsup, face book, twitter, Instagram, Mobile, computer, digital revolution, and Nano or bonsai of everything.

Homes within home-hierarchal and lateral both in dimension and diametrically opposed to each other as well. Parallelism of unparalleled! Without walls, and the inhabitants co-opted with virtual selves and family space. No kids till 40s! The best if no kid at all! The other modern culture is flooding the earth with their respective sons and daughters of gods, to make whole world theirs.

This is typical of us moderns! We say no kids, while others are child producing machine, out to make world crowded with respective dominations! We preach peace, non-violence, freedom and democracy, and we are more violent, freedom has become a sort of fetter! While democracy is gasping for breath on many fronts, we are going gaga over it.

The wars, genocide and mayhem by the moderns have been unprecedented in scale, number, intensity and brutality. Even tribal record would pale before ours! Since we are modern, does it more in all respects. The tribalization of modern and the modernization of tribal ethos and credos! But the test tube baby, IV and surrogacy are also there. Despite the fact that Kids are considered hindrance to free and unbound enjoyment of life.

Here, in our modern homes, we do not seem to be living. We just come to rest and sleep probably. Our respective homes have shifted to diverse one: Virtual corner, multiplicity of personalities, beings, life styles, no hold barred hangouts, and outdoor life! Our shadows live. They become active at day, we at night.

When Sun is up, we drop dead like shadow or invisible, metaphorically and literally as well. Knowledge has been cancelled, soul has been denied, and consciousness and inner self has been denied. On that debris existential and otherwise hollow freedom, multiplicity and pluralism has been built like house of cards amidst shifting sands. Though these are visible to the self yet remains invisible to world. We like darkness—desire, dream, to reek and chill in all and with all without any restriction. No ifs and buts, no good or bad carping, morality and social norms blabalaa.

Sun-knowledge, soul are anathema to us. They force us to be within boundary, to warn and guide they say but is sort of interference to us, it is best that our immediate predecessor-postmodernists have canceled, what is said in Hindi: if no bamboo tree, there will be no flute! The voice of inner self, this consciousness seems to have been lost in infinite space of thoughts, desires and cravings. This is the life that is also the life. Everything and everyone is the life. Live them!

No bad no good things exist in reality. They are what they are: we tag them with good or bad. So it is better to have no judgment, and not being judgmental or soul searching. Keep on going without any hangover, pangs of pain and repentance comes and goes out. What matters only pleasure, a good and free life at our whims and fancies all that counts! We could extract pleasure even from pain like woman getting pleasure from pain!

But the cat fight had started between us: 'you stole him, raped him, I did not like you acting like woman. U have become homo. You are pervert. Blabalaa ....!

Then there was ceasefire. But Cold war persisted. We were unable to make love normally. She was ok but for me third party had become must like appetizer of foreplay! When she came to know, her face glowed and then remained glowing indefinitely.

One afternoon we are simmering with unbound desires and cravings. Both were naked and trying to make love. But we were unable to make any substantial inroads. She would become so hot that it started burning her. No extinguisher was there. In anger and frustration she had gone to balcony. Naked as she was, she would lie down on the reclining chair. I had tiptoed and taken position to watch her unseen.

Her eyes were shut. She was fantasizing and doing the act virtually. In balcony! As if she were challenging the outside to come inside! Even I got excitement at that, seeing her fantasizing! I could bet she was re-living her hilarious escapades with the guy! She had been virtually possessed and taken over by the guy. The cooing and mooning sounds of 'o baby you are great' were sounding familiar! Even I was doing the same.

Then a wall painter doing his work in our adjacent bungalow got a chance peek in our balcony. He had found her naked and a sort of masturbating. The painter was in early 20s. Leaving his work in mid air, he would sit on the ladder decked to the wall. Gazing on the naked beauty of my live in partner lying on the easy chair, he too had started doing some monkey business. He was fantasizing all sort of things perhaps in sequel to fantasying naked beauty!

When she opened her eyes, their eyes met. He winked trying to steal his look from her. But she got beholden by him. She called him. Thinking it might be for someone else, he pretended as if did not notice.

Then she again called him. The young painter boy jumped into balcony. And she pounced upon him like hungry tigress on prowl. I felt a stab in my chest and appeared as if woman inside me would be taking shape,. What she was doing with young painter boy was not her, I felt as if I were doing: mounting straight over him and going on for pleasure trip.

When I came to love sight, the boy got afraid. She soothed him.

'Let's come inside. Babe! I suggested patting both of them.

'Just go away …do not disturb. She would keep on making love brazenly in open balcony naked and made boy also naked tearing down his clothes in tatter. These were scattered all over balcony. The persuasion and pleadings would be all in vain! When she had one orgasm out of the multiple she used to have, only then she relented.

The boy was asked to have bath. The horny slut that she had become wanted to accompany him even to the bathroom. The boy was from Nepal and fair with good physique. She had become mad. Me too! Even the woman inside me had seemed to be getting fresh lease of life!

While Nepali boy was bathing, we had great sex. It appeared our love and marriage life had become dependent on other. It was other that would provide ignition. She had been defiled and I was defiling the defiled! But my male part had got subdued and woman inside me was taking shape. I started feeling more like woman when she was with other. I felt jealous of her and wanted to dismount her from her mount over the lover and to take love ride myself!

I had to go office. And leaving them with heavy heart at home I went to office, but unable to concentrate on work. Mind was there. I was feeling jealous of my partner, envious of her having all of that of handsome and stout boy alone. Like woman I was envying her bliss. What is happening to me! Am going mad or abnormal, I got confused, taking leave from office a bit early.

At home it was theatrics at climax! I felt a stab of jealously that she was having nice time and I left out in lurch was nursing a grudge like horny woman on prowl would sneak into the vantage position, partaking that sight of copulation. That should have been mine—from both point of wife-husband and wife. But surprisedas I would be that my woman half inside was feeling more agreed. Never mind the woman inside was enjoying, while the husband of my live in partner had been lost somewhere in the wilderness of dark passion!

After climax, exhaustion had set in. They went for the deep sleep. I would sneak into and like fox pounced upon the hunt left out by the lioness. I would be replicating what the live in partner had done. I would be following her in the same way my woman inside had not failed to notice. Her ideal was the live in partner-Kajal . So two sluts were out, to devour the life that had come in the form of this handsome and stout Nepali boy.

While the woman inside me was on climax and it was my turn to enter. He got pain, shrieking and waking her up fully. When she came to realize the situation, then all hell broke loose. The fury of woman even the woman inside me could not withstand. I scouted for the safety. In this melee poor guy had sneaked out from our clutch.

3

After the Nepali guy had sneaked out, there was ruckus at home. She was just uncontrollable, getting hysteric and mad. She appeared to have become nymphomaniac. Even Lolita could not have come anywhere near to her cravings perhaps! She was accusing me of having become homosexual. I was denying. It was just woman inside me honey! I knew I was on sticky ground.

But one had to cover his or her ground. The compromise formula arrived on. We should keep male paying guest acting as other to our life. She liked my idea, it was a permanent solution, at least seemed so at that time. But she put a derider: no homo gimmick... only straight n 3s.

'But babe its no homo, it is woman inside me, it's a sort of the love of love for you , becoming one....feeling same .... With you an existential union....

'Please ... leave this rubbish. You have turned homo...

accept man!

'It's not that …its rather hetero-sexual …

But she was not listening. She remained stuck to her ground, as I to mine. She would start fantasizing the future paying guest. We had put the advertisement in the media. Guys would start coming, mostly students. She had singled out one handsome, stout and stud type Punjabi guy. I could not but admire her slightness. She was getting harder to satisfy her, women inside me getting boosted but husband was looking up for prospect of more 3s and 4 s.

Two or three days went by. The Punjabi guy in early 20s arrived as our paying guest. She and she inside me and the hubby had been looking forward to his arrival. There was double whammy: not able to make love and unable to find other as well. Both were to be materialized with. The partner was happiness knowing no bound and limitations. When the guy informed about his arrival, she turned rather hyper as well as the girl inside me!

She had put on special dress for the special Occasion! A see through skimpy red lingerie! At first and subsequent glances she was almost naked: her sexy curves, and roundness, throwing voluptuous aura with prospect of bumpy ride almost visible and feasible. Maddening sort of things Indeed! What would happen when the young paying guest would see her, thinking it the gal inside me blushed and husband blinked. What would happen to wife when I was blushing: she was fantasizing about him! On sofa: in drawing room, almost naked.

There was a ring of door bell. She rushed. He entered. I saw from bedroom unseen. Here would come the guy: 6 feet, fair, sexy with muscles and tattooed as if coming straight from man parlor. Fresh and ready for action! Welcome. She hugged him. Both remained for do not know how long! When they were separated for few seconds, she would again pounce on him, lying down on carpets beneath. Both were more than aroused.

But the guy came out no longer he entered. The slut was unsatisfied and wounded like wounded lioness, starting reviving him. The guy was not relaxed. He seemed a bit afraid of being caught by the husband. She was getting frustrated then I entered to help her. How to revive him, but he got scared, whatever had come up from 15 minutes of labor got further soiled. He refused to put up for her.

I took him to him to his new room asking him to get fresh. But what to do with horny and unsatisfied partner! She was feeling let down by the premature fall of the guy. We were for nice session after her new toy had failed her, feeling rather saddened for the fallen guy.

But the fallen guy further faltered, flunking to be our paying guest. And our adorable other! He had also sneaked before the morning turned off the lights and dark embers of passion!

4

End of paying guest part 1. Part 2 had just begun: the incorrigible and indefatigable partner of mine, and equally selfish hubby craving for bi fling. Out to satisfy his incorrigible libido with her unwed partner. He initiated but now she had started taking the lead. But did it matter whether butter on knife or the knife on the butter! Both were one: I loved her and she loved me, in our own ways, though manufactured truth, norms and regulation.

Everything seemed to be belonging to ours and we are for everything and everyone. There is no other for us!

This time we thought it to keep matured paying guest, rather young and novice who would go away, leaving us thirsty. But one afternoon was something else in store for us! An African young boy turned up to be our paying guest, with all credentials and documents. It was like asking for the moon had been realized. At least for my partner, but not less for me!

The African student was stout and strong with eyes piercing the whole being and even going beyond it. With thong showing normally but after seeing the partner in skimpy see through lingerie, it soon acquired threatening prospect of bursting out of its caged being, but he had put out his hand over it. Even gal in me blushed. Forget my partner! She was just oozing out of way that I did not fail to notice. She was in her favorite see through skimpy lingerie. She specially used to put on to greet such guest. And usually on such auspicious occasion!

I confessed her when she was making tea for African boy—do not get desperate. Wait lest he too ran way like Punjabi guy. She understood and just served the tea with all formality. Sitting beside me instead between us she seemed to have agreed to our plan. Slow and steady. Let him relax, feel at home. No doubt that we are to use him. Let him take initiatives or force him to have her in accident way. So that we could pressurize to do our biddings, dark and golden desires. Woman inside me and hubby as well were just more than hopeful.

But she was desperate! While we slept after failed orgasm and failed erecting. Unsatisfied and insatiate that she was. While an African hunk or stud is sleeping Just across the room, with huge assets. May be for me, it swelled seeing me, the boy concealed, she was thinking as woman or man-woman both, like a sort of Ardhnariashawar (half male and female) inside was also thinking on same line.

When I tried to feel her in semi dark bedroom, she was not there. She was gone. Where? To his room perhaps! I rushed down to his room. She was standing at the door step of African guy suit: naked staring at thongs of sleeping black beauty. I too stopped and took vantage position. But she seemed to be transfixed, her body quivering with bursting excitement. She seemed to be masturbating, seeing sleeping stud in his jockey brief with thongs about to worst from its caged abode. It was as if she was awaiting so to happen.

Taking vantage position I too started following her in the dark fantasies. She was fantasizing naked at the door step of Black young stud sleeping in undergarment. The night was filled with its eerie silence. All movement seems to be happening stealthily all around in the stealth of night.

Only the eerie silence appeared cutting the silence of night, with prospect of a lot of happenings, cheating and co-opting others and risking everything to enjoy the dark passion. I was cheating and sinning on two counts: cheating to myself and partner and husband. Woman inside me was overshadowing man and husband. I was being cheated in consent by two side. One by partner and other my self-woman in me was overcoming the man.

From distance and amidst hazy darkness, African boy also appeared masturbating: she at doorstep of him n he on bed. It seemed imminent that she would plunge into bed. Or he would pounce over her, with vigor and passion. Whichever way it might be, it would be a zero sum game for me. Head and tail both mine!

But nothing happened. Instead a cat crisscrossing near where I was rather hiding created commotion. Kajal woke up from her reveries and dark fantasies. Dark fantasy! Craze among European and American and Asian as well about their prized assets crossing two digits. Initially I thought she would grab it the moment hunk had entered our house. When she did not do, and then thought she would do any time.

The college boy was scared too. He was caught masturbating on my naked partner at his doorstep. While partner was caught doing so by me, and I was caught by her on tom-toting her. Even her fantasies and psychosomatic activities had not reached to its logical end. But his assets were revealed in its full bloom. I put her skimpy lingerie on her while she put that huge back to its abode, while he was pretending to sleep. While she pretended to resort back the displaced entity from its abode, I bet she had fondled it moaning silently that only I listened.

But she had turned hysteric by the passion and hunger of flesh. Seeing no other option, we were out at night. In search of some late night swinging party or swap party or group gang bang party.

5

Its night out there! Dark belly of nature! Wherein darkness and dark forces would appear to be simmering in the dark shadows of the dark jungle that the metropolitan city. Unseen and unheard things might be happening. Dark forces and dark desires were intermingling and finding their fullness and life in the dark. Hunter of all types would be on prowl for the preys to be hunted.

But like jungle preys were not hurrying, scurrying, frenzying, scouting for the safety. Not afraid to be hunted, they seemed to be waiting for the hunter to be preyed upon. For them to be preyed, to be hunted was what they thought as the life and the life style. To be preyed, hunted, to be slave, satisfied like pig in the mundane, profane and routine happiness of life.

But it is post-postmodern world man! The urban and rural jungle meeting on the same dark under belly of roads and fields! It is not darkness. It is light entombed into darkness. It is rather absence of light. When darkness meet the darkness, there arises light of pleasure and pain-mostly of love, sex and deceit, conceit, treachery, and promiscuousness and cheating with consent. It has heralded bilateral, trilateral and multilateral cheating, deceit and debauchery.

But it is not so for us, the post-postmodernist or ultra modernist. Or modern tribal from hindsight! It pertains to logical fallacy of the age: how do you view! It may be treachery and debauchery from society and world point of view. But we don't think so. Had it been so we-generation X! Y! And Z. or XYZ+++ would not have done these. It is ours doing! It's our truth! It's our world, and our life!

Preys wanting to be preyed upon! Hunters craving to be hunted! Its matter of choice, to feel we are free and to reek in reeks like geek! Dream and adventure! To think is to exist. We reek therefore exit. We break all barriers, therefore we exist! We fornicate therefore exit. We slut, do whoring; do abnormal things to feel normal. Even normal and abnormal divide line has been blurred, stretched to the extent where everything is normal, even abnormal!

Preys wanted to be preyed. Look at the live-in partner and me! She in very skimpy n see-though lingerie. On front seat! Spreading her long legs wide open, she looking forward passionately to be preyed upon. And I was driving along with her. And Giving her a poke, a smooch whenever any car passing from opposite direction or overtaking us! Cars halting, screeching, sudden break, and the partaking of unfolding and inviting passion!

We had stopped near a hotel. She asked the guys in SUVs: is there any party going on?

The guys gave shrill and joyous cry at once, in unison.

Yeah man…come we are going there!

We followed them, out to the outskirts. Farmhouse party was on a lonely stretches. Then follow farmhouse. One of 3 big boys would be beckoned by Kajal into our car, just to have the feel of party. The all big boys were drunk and were coming from some party. They were tired and exhausted. Seeing us particularly Kajal in see through sexy dress, they got pepped up.

We reached at the party venue. It was a farmhouse of one of the guys. We had anticipated as to what would happen! Rather it appeared as it were we who had planned it, without our knowing It just happened. All guys were leering at her and she was giving in more than they were asking. I knew she was itching for gangbang sort of things!

Before we parked our car, the party was on. Boys with wine bottle in hands were dancing. Seeing us they all, three encircled us. Dancing and dancing. Live-in partner was in full bloom. One boy started kissing her, other smooching and third tried to assault her swinging hips from behind. But she not taking it that way. Neither do i. We are out to enjoy. she should have what I could not give, but we wanted it, to make it like we are living. She disappeared with him towards swimming pool. I could see her and him. She did it deliberately so that I could also invoke my woman sexuality.

Rest of us would keep on dancing…music. Wine, booze, Ah oomph of Kajal! Shrill cries of remaining boys waiting for their turn, feeling what she might be feeling. Having outdone what partner did to them. Nasty sort of things of big boys! Lot of noise and show of, but no substance! But she knew how to make best out of it. It seemed unable this time as she came with the boy with, bang..bang.….fizz tag line on partner face. I could not fail to chuckle and Kajal could not fail to notice.

The other boy had taken out his asset, beckoning her to have. She started to welcome it. But I told to go in where she had with first boy. I knew soon it would be; bang..Bang fizz. That was what happened with second boy. And third one as well! Party finished as all three boys were finished. But she had not! A burning red rose as if it had further whetted her thirst and hunger.

I suggested a gang bang with me ring master. The boys along with Kajal got excited giving shrill and joyous cries. And party resumed. Gang bang.3, 4 s and all sort of things, directed by the live in husband, woman inside more than hubby, starring the horny and slutty live in partner and three big boys!

And it was not less big time! The live in partner was actress of three dimensional pleasure of gang bang. I had noticed since that day… at policemen party ….as punishment. She had developed liking for it. She got it. And now her thirst was pepping up. We should move out. But I also partook, taking quick shots at all boys as hubby and as gal like what she was doing with them. Before her eyes and along with her! I knew it could be only way to dissuade her from asking more and more, trying to take more out of every Dick and Harry. But was not smuttiness I unfairly used, I was also pimp in that sense. If she whorled… craving more and more…

After I managed to disentangle her from the party, it was 3 of clock of night. Bee hours: Virile and fresh air and aura of pre-dawn! I was driving and she sitting beside me hardly a brazier type top and no panties or lower. No outer, It was I who suggested to take feel in what other might be having. We were happy. She seemed to be happy too, but not showing, hidden behind the cravings and wanting more!

The prey started again to be preyed! Kajal had started waving and throwing flying kisses on passing cars and other one coming from opposite direction.. Stop babe, its vulgar. They would think we are whore and pimp. But it was not whoring: a sort of enjoyment for her! And in that that gusto, she was throwing a flying kiss to the overtaking Tempo traveler. The fellow driving had come to the screeching halt. Then after coming parallel to our car, he replied her flying kiss!

Then taking out a gun and pointing at me, he said: park car aside. Just come to our vehicle. Then he pulled Kajal to his vehicle, clawing her like eagle

I parked my car aside and boarded theirs. They were dacoits or rapists, could not know. But they were not good fellows.

6

When I boarded their vehicle, the stud at driving seat was enjoying with Kajal. And she too! I patted both of them in approval. The cheering and jeering sound followed from rear. Four goons were seated across on 2 x2 seats. So we had been abducted by the gang of five ruffians!They were waiting for their turn.

After I came, the stud took Kajal to the rear, on to bed joined by two seats and drew the curtains. The shouts and cries of rest of four followed: boss hurry up. Its my turn. No mine. No mine.

A fight had ensued among the four goons. The fifth one came out leaving her behind as they werefighting. Kajal would sneak into darkness. I also de-boarded and followed her. We reached our car parked aside the highway. I drove out of fear and safety for our life. We stopped at nearby five star hotel and decided to hide in its Pub.

It was almost 4 o clock. The five star hotel pub remains open 24x7. We could hang out there till things cooled down. Music was wafting across the lounge when we neared it. It was very nice pub. At least 8 or 9 people were there. Notable among was an American who winked at Kajal when we entered. He also gave a friendly sort of smile to me.

He was sitting on right corner. She decided to sit on the side facing him and I facing her. After ordering beer we started enjoying the dreamy aura of pub. Music was ringing the air. Smoke and perfume was wafting, and the people were laughing and talking. The Bar gal was dancing.

After guzzling two or three pint of beer, Kajal had become just jovial. She was trying to get hold the attention of American hunk . He was handsome and stout with tattoo carved, from head to foot. He seemed to be some or other sort of star!

I excused her for washroom. When returned she had hopped to his table, busy in the some peppy talks. The slut still wanted more! Seeing me she would call to their table. He introduced himself: a porn star form US. She just cried: oh porn star. In the ensuing excitement she had leaned on him as if she would sit in his lap. I got a stab in the stomach with a fear she might be lost. But it was only a thought.

But she had hold his hand and her legs were clasped with his under the bar table. Then she would put her right hand under the table and started stroking his thong. Oh she was lusting him. And he was more than responding. It seemed they might start a session right out there in pub.

'where are you staying, she cooed.

'Here right in this hotel, the porn star said

'This hotel…. She gave a cry. but I have not seen any five star hotel room

'It's not room babe. Its suit.

She just jumped as if she would fall swooning on him

'Would you show me?

'Why not ..come.

They just melted away, leaving me to fend for myself. And many raised eyebrows to reckon with.

I waited for a while. Then 10 or 20 minutes elapsed, she did not turn up. I know they won't come. Its futile to be here. I headed home, leaving her with porn star.

But I did not know then that it would be the last of encounter.

After reaching home, I just slept the whole day. She came around evening and slept. Bu when I woke up late in evening. I did not find her. I tiptoed to Af boy room. Through half ajar door she appeared mounting over him, then started a sort of phallus worshipping.

Afterwards it became routine. When I was going office, she would be fast asleep. When I would come home in the evening form office, she would be busy with Af boy. Doors of their room would latched from the inside. They were up to something. The most disgusting thing was that she was not speaking to me. Neither allowing me to join the game of love she would be playing with him, nor we were making love.

Ill omens like things and thoughts would start haunting me. Nothing specific, but something was going to happen, something bad, very bad would be weighing on my heart. But one day the secret of her being shut with Af boy would tumble down accidently. That day I had come from the office a bit early. They were shut within room as usual, but forgot perhaps to shut the door. I saw she and he having sex and broadcasting it to net –on some dating sites.

So she had become porn star! That's why star like attitude! Always shooting , hectic shooting and acting schedule! Oh God! why did I not know then?

After exactly two days later, she would elope with American porn star and AF boy, to become porn star.

7

Kajal had deserted me leaving a big void behind her. A void within void! Earlier it was lack of void amidst too much of the actions and activities! I was ruing the void of having no voids! The life with her was like fast cut movie. It was too fast to have void or gaps. Now what she had left behind her was this void of nothingness, a infinite silence of meaningfulness having become meaningless. Cacophony of inner voices was unable to fill up the void. When everything had tumbled, yet it appeared to be going down to nowhere.

What had remained was a baffling loneliness. I was alone in the world, cut off from the family, friends and all those relations much earlier. Now these had started to haunt my loneliness. Even office, professional relations and all networks had been lost. And what could be retrieved was the revolting revolt of the self against itself. The void after hustle and bustle, emptiness, and loneliness was stretching beyond the void without!

I was missing the family life! I wished I would have gone for simple marriage life-arranged marriage. I wished I would not have opted for nuclear family cutting myself from joint family. The Support of family in crisis would have been there! But if it was my option, then why these are being missed now?

It was her life. She thought it would be better with porn star and Af boy. Had I got any such things of my interest, I would have followed her way. But why this self that was remembering all those had remained with big void. As nature abhors vacuum and void, so should I do the same!

So solo indulgences would start filling up this void. Swingers party, Swap, bachelor party, High party and Group party! But these failed initially to swing my mood and hold any interest for long! Fast music, heart thumping scenes: Gals and boys , men and women, elderly and old-- all dancing. Some naked, while most of them almost naked! Rounds, length and width getting mixed with music! Topless and in tattered denim, couples sucked up into each other! Or two males and females for 3 s and 4s: Some doing right there. Booz was oozing. Drugs were drugging up the frenzy and madness. Smoke seemed to be reducing us to the smoked flesh!

It was hazy out there but life seemed to be bustling and bursting forth. Or it was hurtling back to the tribalism of yore: Promiscuousness, group marriage and sex. Everyone free to mate with other one! Then they had started dog fight over it. And at last it had become institutionalized in the form of marriage. As watching this unfolding of the tribal credo from the bar room, it would appear as the tribal redo of the modernity. It seemed rather disgusting, shameless and wildness in sheer carnality at its height. Flesh and flesh only in all tones, color and texture.

What was happening to me! Going nuts…scene was the tribal or seer? The projection of seer or scene! They seemed to be overlapping with other! It was veneer of modernity or that of tribal? Why this contradiction… either its modern or postmodern or post tribal …one couple accosting me…finding alone and gaping depressingly…taking for 3 s… then other for 4s!

The central hall of hotel! Hard music had suddenly stopped. The dancing crowd had fallen silent. Light Music of night was wafting. An African hunk with huge assets seemed to be out on exhibition-cum-buffet party…men and women, young and old, lesbian and gays, hetero and transverse coming and partaking his with a lot of uh and oomph. It seemed strange: tribal. Voodoo and nausea of modernity!

Then a gay couple had grabbed me for experimental performing of 3 s. Afterwards one more gay or some sort of hetero out to enjoy, then other hetero type joining in for 4s. I was just unable to decide my identity! Male or female or gay or lesbian, hetero or transverse! The body was not mine. The gender had embarked on fluid turf becoming indeterminable entity! It was not mine. Everything had changed apparently or in reality, even that kept on changing, apparent becoming the real and the real apparent. From male to female, Gay to hetero and lesbian to 3 s and 4 s, multiple identity and multiple pleasure! This was the life and identity that we moderns or ultramodern or postmodern pining for, I was wondering with disgust and disillusionment.

When I came to home in morning, the morning was no longer morning and home did not look like home. The home appeared to have transformed into a sort of jungle. It is said that without woman a home is like haunted place! But my home seemed to have become haunting place of shadows. The shadows of all sorts were playing shadowing game, overshadowing my whole being and life!

It was being very difficult to decide whether I had lost my sense or submerged with eternity. The self had forgotten itself or had merged with all and one. Whether my being was in comatose or had become self hypnotized, not sure. But it was certain that I had lost my gender and overall identity. The shadows of male, female and transverse were crowding the space left vacant by Kajal!

8

When I left home yesterday, I had lost only Kajal—my live in partner. She had deserted the day before. When returned home that afternoon, I seemed to have lost everything: my identity, my gender, my being and everything that was. A new self had descended to my being. A sort of multiples beings and identity bordering on the split personality had become new narrative. The narrative of changing beings and gender seemed to have become the defining narrative of the moment. Was not its mine choice? A freedom, free choice option to be more living or alive!

After the judgmental night, every barrier and limitations had been shed down. I was more feeling like woman and transgender than the male. My original gender-male was also competing for the attention but it was weak on the ground. One gender was coming after another in succession. Even if it was not normal but abnormality at large, I could not help it. Kajal and her girly things would be appearing more alluring. Even with her, I used to think and feel what she was feeling.

Often we would fight, contest, discuss and mess up on this issue: homosexuality and feeling like woman. She would strongly assert: you are homo, and I would retort rather bluntly: no its woman inside me that was invoked by you to be culprit. But our contentious debate would keep on lingering without any end in sight.

Kajal would often accuse me of degrading the woman. I would refute it vehemently   but not ready to accept myself as homo. Even if it has been legalized and being considered as matter of choice and more so of individual sexuality, I was not willing to accept. Woman part had come into my being having taken shape after our live in marriage. I would be thinking and feeling like woman. Perhaps this might have been one of the reasons for her eloping with two foreigners, without bothering to tell me or inform me!

The homosexuality is no longer considered as abnormal by the moderns. Still the idea did not fit with us. For change or some experimentation, it may be considered as one time aberration but as choice it would never be appealing to me. But Kajal knew it and did not like it. She was jealous like one woman of other. She had always been nursing the grudge of stealing her lover or scaring them away from her.

Now she had gone, but the woman part that she had left behind her in me was there. It was giving succor. As if she was there, even if she had gone. No she was still with me. I am she and now she may not be. But i am her, I was thinking .and after she had gone, it had become more prominent.

Then door bell rang. Who could be in the loneliness of blazing afternoon? I opened the door with horny loneliness of the bored house partner, fantasizing who could give her break from the routine life!

A delivery guy of online shopping agency: stout man with dark complexion, he was average in look. But look hardly mattered to lonely and horny woman! For that matter to horny man as well.

'Come inside, it's very hot outside. She in me had started casting net!

'It's ok, he said wiping his sweating forehead.

'Do come and have a glass of water. It was sweltering heat; she in me had started plotting.

Sweating profusely he would come inside. My heart started beating like hers in expectation! It had started choking with excitement, gasping for breath.

'You are married, I asked offering him a glass of water.

'Yes, he said rather awkwardly

'How long?

'Five years..

'Any kid

'No kid…some problem partner

'Oh then you must be having problem

'But you look quite healthy and virile.. . started touching all over him, his thong was swelling.

'Problem with partner?

'Yeah..

But it might be yours…. . opening zips of his pant. There came out his with ready to enter into any challenge.

Holding in my hand and fondling it said: you are virile and sexy..problem must be with her.

And I was re-living Kajal in me: what and how must be she feeling and doing sort of things. I was just imitating and imagining her. I was her, my live in partner in reality who had deserted, but she had resurrected in me.

This abnormality could not keep me alive beyond certain time and situation. Afterward of such homosexual encounter, being camflouged under 'woman inside me 'or 're-living the Kajal , followed an intense bout of inner conflicts. There would start the hours of self-loathing and hatred for my being. Even If it has been legalized and considered normal things, then why there is intense bout of depression, self loathing and a feeling of nauseas sort of things, I would often think with pain and agony.

Then I again and again would lapse in the reveries of her! The empty home deserted by Kajal often would revive her memory…That day when she was with me and toy… or that man or woman, black guy, white man. All would be whirling past me like film reels in fast cut. But the feeling of the reeking abnormality in my being would not relent down a bit. It would be followed by the guilt of not doing justice to the original self and gender.

Then there would start the mania for cross dressing! Always in her dresses and undergarments, I would be taking delivery boys and other men of daily uses in my net. The net would be woven around the story of a journalist working on thematic inquiry on the average size of adult male. It would be for some obscure non-existing journal or Men's Magazine. And lo and behold it would become quite a hit. And it had become quite successful as well, with failure rate very minimal.

After exhausting this alibi, hunt would start for fabricating another mode. The resurrected woman and reunited live in partner inside me was craving for more. Variation, some hardcore act of love, 3s 4 s type that used to fascinate had started bumping me, giving gooseberry.

My being seemed to have become playground of three beings or three genders: self, deserted live in partner and perverted being-transverse. Split personality. Changing like chameleon. Three genders I would live, seeking merely carnal pleasure or filling the perceived or unperceived lack. The self and its being would crisscrossing from male to female to transverse. Was it for pleasure or had become necessity to go on living. Perhaps very reason for being remained alive!

Morning usually would start with self flogging, a lot of remorse, self loathing and antagonistic protest against the life and its moments and instances. Then would follow the action, to sooth the bruised ego and low esteem resulting from self battering itself. This would lead to the switch over to woman self and then it was free for all. It had become a sort of vicious circle of abnormality

Even if the modern society and modernity has permitted such aberration, then why I would have this self-loathing, and feeling of doing something wrong? Is it only conditioning and what moralists of society say as wrong that is reason for such self-flogging? Either I am wrong or this abnormality! I would often think in vain.

Could a thing wrong in one age, a particular time and space be right in other ones? If it is so, then why should i have such debilitating disability and inertia of mind and body as if it were the virtual death or the end of things! If wrong things would be becoming right with a change in time and space, then does not it imply that there are no good and bad things? It is only matter of convenience of time, space and individuality perhaps! Or this is what modernity or post modernity or post-postmodernist stands for! I could not help myself from arriving at any conclusion.

Be what whatever be! It was Sarah, Kajal friend, who would help me to wade out of this a sort of vicious circle of my being and life!

9

One day Sarah visited our residence. Her visit came like a straw of hope to the drowning man. She would take me back to the shore of life from mid stream where Kajal had left after deserting me for the greener pasture. It was she who would put me back to the semblance meaning in life that had turned meaningless. She was the friend of my live in partner, Kajal. She was trying to contact her but was unable to do so for a few days. How could she? She was not aware that she had left the country for good, deserting me and all that was her.

When Sarah could not see Kajal, she asked about her whereabouts. I could only say she was not at home. She slumped down on sofa, saying, oh God!

'What happened? I asked.

She started crying. Something wrong seemed to have happened. After consoling her and offering a glass of water, she regained a semblance of normality.

'What s matter Sarah?

'Jeb-my husband has become homosexual and has deserted me, said she resting her head on my shoulder.

I was shocked. Having seen me so, she fell silent as if she should not have confided her problem to me.

Now it was my turn to shock her.

'But Kajal has deserted me. She has not become Lesbian but a porn star in US.

Now it was her turn to be shocked. Hence would start a doomed courtship based on shock , agony, madness and pain of desertion by respective spouses.

3
SARAH AND JEB

Sarah and Jeb were couple of the mixed race. Her husband-Jeb was West Asian Christian, settled in India. And Sarah hailed from Hyderabad, belonging to erstwhile obscure Nawab family. She was beautiful loaded with perfectly shaped figure of a hot actress. At first instance, she would be looking like chiseled Greek beauty and when looked from near she would appear Indian beauty with heavy bosom, narrow waistline hosting sizeable hips. And her husband was equally well built and handsome.

They were a tad bored of having the routine life and act of love. Sarah wanted to have some change of taste so that it could pep up their southward going marriage life. She would talk about these things, but Jeb showed rather restrained interest, as his wont, he with low sex drive would consider it as necessary evil. But forSarah it was necessary evil for staying put alive. And she had been with very difficulty sticking to Jeb. Many times, she would feel like leaving him and going for some stud.

But better sense would prevail. She had planned to have extra fling and kinks within marriage, roping in Jeb as well . First it started at fantasy level during act of love making. Then why not go for once at least. But Jeb would be dead against it initially. He had said, it was ok at fantasy level, but going for it in reality was a risky proposition.

He would say: I won't allow you to be touched by other. Sarah would feel like she was losing out life and its enjoyment slipping breath by breath. But she was not one to relent on so easily.

She along with him had put themselves on dating and the adult dating sites. They would be scouting other social media and networks. She would start showing him porno during the act of love. But he would not be warming up. Then she would go for the track 2 of trapping diplomacy. One day when he was unable to hold for long, she suggested him to take some sex boosting medication. He used to have loose erection and pre-mature ejaculation would be norm with him. He would let her down during the climax and peek.

' Honey! You should try some tonic….. She had said hesitatingly lest he took it as affront to his manliness

Jeb did not respond.

'Or should take Viagra…..check with some sex expert.

First it was big no, then relented a bit.

' you are ok…. We need some variation..you would bring some toy for me.

'Toy?

She showed a video of a husband bringing a toy-a black man with huge assets. And both making love with her. Seeing this, the cold hubby had got very passionate making passionate love. Sarah concluded: the very idea has brought back life in our life…what would happen when we did it…..

Then started the hunt for toy! Jeb had conceded to it rather skeptically. He remained cold to the idea outwardly but inwardly getting pepped up. Sarah had not failed to notice his excitement and erection at the very idea for toy for her. It appeared to her it would click with him, giving her immense joy and excitement.

Both would be putting the advertisement on different dating and adult dating sites. They also opened their accounts with them, putting some intimate pictures of both as profile and album. It had become instant hit and hordes of replies and response began to pour in. She was overwhelmed and he too seemed to be happy about it.

Afterwards they would startthe process of sorting out the offers. They zeroed-on few toys initially. She wanted to plunge head on in this pleasure. She was dying for having nice and long session with a stud and hunk type guy. Jeb was very short lived in love session and did not make efforts . Now her wait was coming to an end.

She would start in the interview and the real time meet. The proposal for toys kept pouring like incessant rains. Sarah had secret plan as well. She would be enjoying all the 10 toys they had short listed for 10 days.

There came the first toy- A Punabi guy. In early 20s with good physique , tall and handsome. This toy gave Sarah goose bumps. But Jeb objected it for no sufficient reason. She knew he would do it.

When Jeb was away at office, she would call the toy no 1 and toyed with him. It was very nice. She felt as if she had got new lease of in the life gone dull and staid. But when Jeb would reject the second and third toy as well, she got suspicious. She did it with the second also and the third toys as well, in his absence when he would be at the office. How would it matter when he had agreed in principal to have toy for me. He had changed later on. Let it be.

She would enjoy, Sarah had decided.

The last of toys to be interviewed and interacted was a black guy , with huge thong. When Sarah met him, she had fallen for him at the first sight. Jeb as usual would not like him, but Sarah would become a sort of hysterical about him. Incidentally Jeb had to go on official tour for few days. Perhaps for this reason he might have rejected the toy. But Sarah for the same reason had accepted it secretly. And she had called him when Jeb was on the official tour.

The toy and his assets were marvelous. She would keep and play with him till Jeb was on tour. The three nights and two days, with that toy! It was hilarious experience to be cherished for life time.

The escapade that she had with Punjabi guy and black one would even bowl me over! She told everything about her long session with black boy, almost three nights and 4 days. She would tell and confide every details; the most interesting was the role playing of LGBTQ: Lesbian, gay, bi-sexual, Transverse and Questioner or quasi type. It would be better if her confession is given attention to in her own words.

4
CONFESSION OF EVE

I was on the seventh heaven when the Punjabi guy entered home that afternoon. We -I and my hubby were interviewing online and offline—real time as well 10 guys to be one of them as my toy. I had shortlisted it and secretly desiring to play with all10 toys. I knew Jeb had agreed reluctantly to it. As he was unable to satisfy and satiate my hunger and thirst, he had no other option. He was well aware that I might quit the marriage if he tried to act obstinate.

The first toy I liked very much. With his entry I was his. Jeb had also noticed it, with some sort of jealousy . He did not like the way my whole body was baying for him. That is why he rejected first toy I wanted to play with. It hurt me so badly I thought quitting him. Then I decided its better to do it secretly. It would not be categorized as cheating. As Jeb had agreed to have toy for me, no issue on that.

I did not know why I had inkling that Jeb would be rejecting all the toys. Agreeing to it was perhaps his tactical move. He seemed to be playing for time being or asking for time. Or awaiting some opportune time he knew it best. But why should I miss this golden opportunity.

The moment I called that guy, he came no soon than that was expected. As if he was ready to be called upon. When he rang the door bell, I was in bathroom. When opened door in bathrobe-a towel around, he got turned on. So much that we made first round of love at the doorstep. Then we went to bedroom and oh God! He was so hot. Likewise I enjoyed all 9 toys and 10th was a black guy.

This guy-black guy changed everything. As Jeb had gone on official tour for four days, we had all time. For four days, he had shifted to our house. And it was marathon. He took me to ultimate pleasure and a heaven not heard so far. A heaven of LGBTQ!

'LGBTQ…. ? I could not check myself from interrupting Sarah.

'Lesbian, gay, bi-sexual, transverse and questioning or questioner of this life style, Sarah said with gesture and posture as if she if she were role playing

'Life style….

'Yes it has become a life style.. It started with movement for legal and non-legal right for lesbian and gay and transverse. Now it has become life style..a craze …

Sarah was back to confession trail, interrupted by my curiosity inadvertently.

Well, when black stud told me about LGBTQ, I could not understand initially. Then he would introduce me to this life style. After nice and exhilarating session with his huge assets, we would start the role playing these five life styles!

First we would play the role of lesbian. He would become woman and we would start donning the role of lesbian couple. He would make the love like a woman did to other woman. I would use a toy for his and he also did the same. I had really enjoyed playingthe lesbian.

Then he taught me how to play the role of homosexual. He asked to feel like man and handed me masculine toy to consummate my new-founded manhood. And we enjoyed man to man sex as we did during woman to woman. It was really an experience to transform into man and enjoy their sexuality.

Then bi sexual role! I did girly thing to him and he did same sex with me. We exchanged our role as per our convenience. Then we both transformed into role of transverse after feeling deprived of normal sexual relations. We artificially decapitated our respective sex organs to have the feel of a transverse enjoying his or her sexual individuality.

Then the black guy was teaching to don the role of questioning. But Jeb barged into our world having cut short his tour. He became so angry that he kicked the black guy in the wee hours of night. And we have a nice fight. Then it was followed by passionate love making!

1

Jeb would be grumpy and sore. The ceasefire had been announced and patch up had been worked out. Even then he was always ready to pick fight. He could not forgive the agreed upon cheating. The only wrong was that I did it alone without taking him into confidence. To make it up, I offered a way out: we should find toy for him. This cheered him up finally. It had appealed to him as befitting equalizer.

Thence had stated our mission to find a toy for Jeb. First we loitered around restaurants, mall, known hook up sites and market places. In one restaurant, one gal was eying Jeb. She was sitting alone across the two tables. I noticed Jeb was also taking interest in her. She could be nice toy for him, I decided.

We had shifted to her table. When we had settled down her table, I went to washroom and took enough time. So that Jeb could have enough time and space to strike some sort of engagement with her.

When I came back, Jeb and the gal were engrossed in some peppy talks perhaps. When they saw me coming, she tried to be formal. But Jeb was soothing her ruffled feathers. When rejoined them, my hubby seemed to have won over toy for him.

But Jeb lost his booty on bed. In my presence he failed to prove himself. Poor gal, I empathized with her. I could understand her agony of left out with fire with empty fire extinguisher. But I soothed her with lesbian role that my Black booty had taught me. And interestingly Jeb was stealing eye on us making love with each other. And I found him fondling himself!

After this fiasco of toy unable to be toyed with, we decided to go for couple. And we shortlisted a couple with perfect assets: gal having Lopez like gyrating ass. It would give Jeb immense pep up that I did not fail to notice. As per their adult dating site profile, they were in 30s. Partner was Punjabi and hubby a handsome South Indian guy. He was working in MNC. His partner was socialite and frequenter of the adult dating sites. Broad shouldered decked with large and conical shaped breast, big eyes and sensuous lips! She was enough to make dead body alive!

We sent our profile and some pictures in exchange for theirs. The date and venue was decided and his partner was taking the lead. So I thought our mission for Jeb's toy would be successful. But I did not have an iota of doubt that it would prove rather cataclysmic for our life.

'What happened? I could not help but ask Sarah about it. The way she told fuelled my curiosity.

'I will tell you. Sarah continued her erotic reminiscences. When I and Jeb entered their abode as agreed upon, they were dressed in their undergarments only. I could not but find myself lost in her matchless beauty and sexy figure. And she also appeared to have fallen for me.

We have hardly settled that she would start playing with me, Instead of Jeb. Jeb and her hubby were just dumb struck seeing us involved passionately in same sex fore play. When they started feeling embarrassed, her hubby took Jeb to his bedroom.

When we were finished with first round of act, I peeped into their bed room. Jeb and her hubby were busy in making love. I again got pepped up and made love with her again. Again and again. They were also playing the roles. Thus Jeb became homo and I lesbian

'Coming to LGBTQ or LGBTQAI…., I had few doubts, wanted to sort out with Sarah.

' LGBTQ.. A..I…, Sarah interjected.

'Its new addition to life style… of sexuality and individuality… Artificial intelligence AI

'yes …yes I heard… she was trying to cover up her ignorance perhaps. But something else was bothering me.

'Don't you think its wrong…,to transform… a movement world over…for rights and respectability of sexually decapitated and deprived group…..to that of life styles and role play for sexual enjoyment..for exploring freedom and individuality.

'What you are speaking is beyond my faculty to understand.. and I don't want to understand I don't care… if it gives enjoyment and meaning in life… so it be, Sarah said in her typical offhand style.

'But what if stuck up in role as you and Jeb been, I wanted to clear some doubts. You both have stuck up in one role. You both forgone your respective gender getting enamored of lesbian and homosexuality..

She fell silent and became very sad. Perhaps I should not have asked it. Sarah had become serious.

Then she left hurriedly. Oh God! I forgot one work…

--Bye…see you soon

-Bye.

I slumped down to sofa. The life ahead had started scaring me. Void and emptiness had again started terrorizing. The life without Kajal did not seem to be worth living. Now Sarah had also left. Even if for us, there is no other. Other is not hell but heaven! To enjoy with, to love and make love! It is they who give me real being. My life ticks through them. Life realizes through them! How could be they 'other'? They are extension of me or you honey!

Life is ticking. Age is catching on, time slipping. Grab what we can: in war n love everything is fair. Love has shifted to the flesh and flesh to the love. Centre becoming periphery making it centre (of attraction) centric. Form, body, flesh, and the multiplicity that is what seems to be sum total of life.

No boundary has remained. All boundaries and limitations

have tumbled down. If they stumble upon, do they certainly, accept as it were not there. With love, happiness, freeing of ego and dissolving it in all that unfold before us.

But Why it is so that life seems nothing without other. When other is there, my being seems to be forgetting itself and submerging with other. When other goes out why this void and emptiness! Are we free or dependent on others! If dependent then how could we claim our self free! I was wondering about the mystery that life is!

2

Other day Sarah had called up. She was throwing a party. She invited me to join. It was good break from my solitude and solo existence. Though alone yet not alone in my world! How could there be anyone alone? He or she could feel loneliness, but never alone. The world and its people, its frills and thrills even if in memory, and in form of any type of thoughts, agony and pain and sorrow always would be crowding the vacuum of existential space. The others might be absent but their presence would be there in form of thoughts of absent. The outside is always inside and inside is the presence of the absent outside!

Sarah invitation reminded the call of outside. It was all inside: the play of memory, gyration of mind, cacophony of thoughts, flights of endless desires, self loathing and self doubt . And then on to seventh heavens! But Sarah brought down to the earth: Inside meeting the outside and merging and becoming a unique moment of inside-outside!

Off to Sarah party. Party of the party! Medleys of party! Swingers, swap, all bachelor or gang bang. Everything was there for all sort of life styles. Role play and reeking in individuality and individual freedom of having all possible pleasure, to squeeze out of the life all its juices! And then there was change in the roles and gender. Why glued to one gender, sex and the being born into. It was not our choice to be born with our gender and being. Now when choice is available, life and its frills providing such a wide range of choices, why not enjoy!

But Sarah had become lesbian and Jeb homosexual. Both unable to enjoy normal and hetro or another roles. So they were busy in finding their own limitations. For me all were open. With open mind and no premeditated agenda, living all and partaking all role plays. Not through active participation, but as indulged observer. As viewer or a voyeurs! A self doubt piercing the heart: whether I have become voyeurs! How does matter, its like lesbian and homosexuality not considered as aberration or abnormality. I was wondering whether voyeurism should be added to LGBTQAI+V or not!

I was hoping that the LBBTQIA people would not get hurt. They are already hurt by high jacking of their movement of rights and acceptability about their plight to the role play groups and their culture. What more could hurt them. But for moderns and post-moderns, it is a sort of bonanza of life styles and role play. To reek in basic instinct and drive have been upgraded to life style, as assertion of ones individuality and sexuality. And freedom to sally forth across gender. Not only change in gender, for fun on snapchat .but real time feel of all possible enjoyment.

While veering and voyeuring around the ongoing party, one couple- Neel and Nili happened to attract my attention. It appeared as if they were look out for me. Then they beckoned. Both were like Ajanta staccato: Greek, Indian and Persian beauty in one. But when I ventured around them, they started making love ferociously. As if there were looking for someone presence to be into love making. That too like long before lost horny couple meeting somehow and somewhere as chance encounter.

Since then, we became friends and I invited them to my home. They readily agreed and after party accompanied me to my desolate nest. They were unable to make love without presence of third person. Third party fixation seemed to have become their woe or a sort of fixation.

'How and when it happened, when asked, they would start revealing their escapades. Predicament or choice or freedom to reek in all sexual individuality. Or unable to make any, and stuck up in some other role!

5
NEEL AND NILY

It so happened that we were unable to make sex for long time. We had two room set accommodation in the suburb. There was no space and privacy for us. Children used to sleep with us. Now they had grown up, further shrinking the space for us. It was difficult to consummate our conjugal freedom. Earlier we would make love in the morning when children were out in school. But ever since our parents had come to stay with us, we lost even that golden moment as well.

One day we decided to check out in a hotel. The hotel was a sort of home stay type of accommodation, very homily. We were more than happy. But soon it turned out to be a night mare. There was a camera secretly placed. We were through with first round of love making. There was knocking at the door. A guy in early 20s had entered with mischievous smile on his face . He appeared to be son of hotel owner.

He showed our love making on his cell phone and tried to blackmail us.

'What do you want? Nily asked wrapping her naked body with bed sheet.

'You , pat came the reply from him

At this she got hysteric .Wriggling her naked body from bed sheet she started making love with me. Right there before him , saying :'watch me u f....r .

After that incident third party presence would become our condition for love making. We did not know then it was called 3 s and what not. We needed someone to enable us to make love.

One evening we were going out for dinner. On the way, around lonely stretch she happened to see a guy easing himself. She got enamored of his asset. She asked me to stop. Indicating towards him, she said: look how great...... . I saw it and even felt like her. When the guy finished, she asked the whereabouts of a place we knew well. She invited him to escort us there. The guy agreed more than willingly.

The moment he entered the car, she shifted to rear seat where the guy was seated. I started observing them from mirror. Foreplay had started. When it became unbearable, I also joined. We made it inside the car. Happily forgetting our dinner as our platters was full with delicious dishes.

On next weekend we went for movie. Only we knew that we were not going to see movies. It was to act it out the third party for us! So that we could make love! It had become rather conditional or rather a sort of obsession to have the presence and participation of other to make our love session successful.

We were rather playing double game of love. Get any hook up for group or gang bang, and of course in addition to our booty of three- four roles playing. Though not consciously, it had just happened. But I did not know then it was rather his plan. We had bought three movie tickets. And we were for the lookout of some stud type guy for hook up. Positioning strategically on a vantage point, we had started keeping watch over the movie goers.

We sorted out a Chinky guy. He was staring her through her see through mini and tops. He had yellow complexion with good body and average height!

We both nodded at each other. Then he went where the chinky was standing in the question for ticket.

'Excuse me we have got extra ticket, i said rather hesitatingly as if gasping for breath. Our friend did not turn up and if you could take it….

'how much I have to pay. Pat came reply from the chunky guy.

' We would settle that later on, I said.

I came back with him to staircase of movie hall where she was sitting. I noticed at least four guys sitting in row on stair just below her. They were staring her rather brazenly. When I followed their eyes, it was to her skirt and beyond. It gave me excitement and feeling of virility rather!

Then I introduced her to him. We had enough time for the show to begin. We went for coffee in nearby shop. Over a cup of coffee the Chink guy had started opening up. He got friendly with us. He was a college student. After break up with his girlfriend, he had come out for the movie.

No sooner movie had started, than they started shooting their own movie. After the initials of kissing and all, they were coming to actual in the movie hall itself. People had started casting side and long glances. I told her: lets go out to some place. And we checked out in a motel and enjoyed our time with that guy.

1

Then we did not realize that third party presence had become a disability! Until one morning, when we would be unable to make love. She was quite horny that morning. But my weapon was surrendering before it would fire any shot. All the efforts to revive it was proving to be unfruitful.

'You have become impotent, Nily blurted out. And I did not take it lightly. There started a prolonged wordy duels and fights. I went out in huff, leaving her horny, unsatisfied and angry with me at home.

It was a pleasant morning! The cool morning breeze was playing music in my ears. I went to Lodhi Garden. There I noticed a tall girl with tons of beauty and sex appeal! She had put me off the hook. I would start following her with intention to strike friendship with her.

The girl was walking briskly with her long legs. Her bottoms were swinging in alluring way. She looked back. She had beautiful face with brown eyes too big to be looked into! I waved at her. She responded with a thin but charming smile! It was obvious she had not come for walks! With heavy makeup and party dress that she was in, she had come for getting hooked up!

I would pace up my walk. After overtaking her, I greeted her. She responded in no uncertain terms of friendship. And I had cast the net of friendship with all familiar dialogues! We decided to sit on nearby garden bench to relish our newly struck friendship. I wanted to prove myself as well as to her that I was not impotent!

After some initial work out, it was no possible to go further in the garden. So we checked in a nearby guesthouse. And I proved that I was not impotent as Nily had alleged. From hindsight it seemed as if it were done for checking my alleged impotency. But when returned home in evening, there was another scenario challenge awaiting there!

She was having it with electrician who had come on call. Out in the bedroom . The door was ajar. The electrician was over the stool kept on the bed for holding the fan. And she was having it. Even when she noticed me coming, she would keep on enjoying with him. The electrician had turned pale with fear. But she soothed him with prolonged French kiss. They had picked up the love act from where it was disrupted.

Afterwards we tried to make it without presence of third party. But it was of no use. Have we turned abnormal or mad or impotent or frigid? Or all, we were not sure. But our life was becoming hell. Seeking presence of other for our love making had become a risky proposition! It had many frightful consequences!

One day we met Abdullah and Ayesha in a party. Abdullah, called Abid was in 60s and Ayesha was in 20s. But her look and appearance was that of the teenagers. Just like Lolita. I had met her first time when Abid had invited some of his close friends to celebrate his fourth marriage.

Abid's three wives had deserted him. The first one left him for his nephew. The other eloped with his driver. The third one was not his type. He with low sex drive, She with high. The marriage was loaded against him with very beginning. And it exploded soon. Then Abidhad decided not to marry again. He wanted to enjoy the rest of his life without partner.

But life had something else in store for him. It so happened that one of the best friends of Abid had died in a plane crash, along with his partner. Only Ayesha had survived as she was having board exam of 12th standard. The community decided that he should marry her. Thus Ayesha became better half part of his life!

That day when Nily saw her, they became very friendly. Leaving us in drawing room, they were having some frequent private moments. And by the time we would leave Abid house, she was in madly love with Ayesha. A lesbian tango had happened.

And I would lose her further. The presence of other had been rendered irrelevant! She seemed to have become full-fledged lesbian!

2

Neel and Nily had left for their home. I was back to square. Empty home was staring with desolation. Kajal had started haunting me in her present absence! The Life was back to monotonous nauseating routine: Office to empty home and back to office where I did not feel like working. Since one has to work to live, I was working.

Back to the Home! Where I did not feel like living in! Since one has to have home to live in, I was coming back to the nest long abandoned by the birds! As one has to live the life, I was living in it. But the life did not seem to be having purpose and meaning!

But another matter was perturbing me. Has the life, for that matter, any purpose and meaning at all! What is happening! What will happen! Why it has happened! The life seemed to be revolving around this narrative! And one day it comes to end with super narrative: what will happen to the life, its meaning and purpose! What remains is a void!

So life is series of voids, I was thinking. And it ends with another void and on and on. Then it enters the big void at the end of its journey.! The work, relationships, time and space melting into that big void! Where they go and from where they come for that matter? To nothingness or void! If these have to go one day, then what they have come for. A conundrum that life is, had started baffling me! Sometimes it looked like meaningful. While other time not. A void, an emptiness. Right now it is here and there. Next moment it has gone! Earlier it has not been there. There is no guarantee that it will be in future.

I was getting depressed. Self-loathing, a feeling as if I had demeaned the self, society and humanity would begin to pin me down. The protest and rebellion against society and its traditions and conventions! Then it was the cause célèbre for freedom! The individual choice and individuality! Now it seemed to have solidified into the guilt and remorse as if something like blunder had happened!

A weight on mind! A feeling crushing and crashing the self: what is meaning of life, of modern life. Or at the best post-postmodern life! Enjoyment in flesh and fornication, fiefdom of carnal and banal call of flesh in all its manifestation and perversion! That is all the choices seem to be available for the individuality and freedom. The all call for freedom and individuality, individual choices and plurality seem to be pattering on this carnal desire and enjoyment.

The cynics may whine bracketing me to the 'Q'of LGBQIA. I don't want to get fixated on any role. It is nothing but seems to be subversion of the movement in course to grant rights and respectability to the sexually deprived and marginalized gender and class. How and when it seems to have become life style statement and role play, a matter of choice and option for individuality and sexuality? I had no idea and neither had I wished to know.

Sometimes it seemed to be so fascinating and pleasure giving, freeing the self from gender and class-color brackets. The madness and frenzy that it gave rise to, would sweep all barrier of ego, limitation of body and gender. Sometimes it seemed as if there were no other. The centre of life seemed to be shifting from the self to other. It was the other that seemed to have become the real self rather. Other would melt into the self and the self would become other. It was a sort of perfect union with world and universe.

In other way: it could be love with all: there is no self as it seems to have become other, while other is the self becoming other. So there does not arise any matter of conflict. But why more often than not feeling of a sort of guilt, doing something wrong creeps in. It might be like birth pang and pain resulting from the transition of one being to other, I was thinking.

As Sarah had told it was becoming in thing. Even though not in open, everyone secretly or otherwise would be doing it. It is matter of individuality, choice, and freedom. Really ...when I heard about it, I felt very elated as if life could be worth living. Despite everything else, if it gives meaning to one life, there is nothing wrong in trying for it. As they say right and wrong, truth and untruth are individual, time and space specific. My truth, it is not necessary that it would be yours or her or his! So be cool and chill!

If am wrong, It might be right for you. And I won't say you are wrong. In same way if there is something wrong for society, then it might not be so for many or individual. So far role plays are considered, these are individual choices, but it is understood a threat to our heterosexual culture. But how, I was unable to understand that time. It's another matter that soon I realized its perversity to the peril of my very existence.

For time being, it appeared only condition for living. It seemed to be panacea for my all problems in life. It was staring since her desertion particularly. She was not there yet she was haunting all over. What a predicament! Should I change home? Or gender. Snap chat: great sexy. I can pass the test. Cross dressing. Her clothes fit in. Opening accounts on dating sites! Then live broadcast: IM

'Hi

'Hi a/s/l

'Urs

Couple but partnerseparated ….male

'Same here …partner deserted…

'Thinking to bi

'Great. Me too.

'Size

'8+

'Do you have place

'Nope and u

'Space is the problem..

'Got place…you can come

He or she, not sure, did not turn up. But my few days were pepped up. A new gender, new being and new life had dawned. Not limited by any gender, not restricted to any being. Enjoy life. I would start broadcasting on dating and adult dating sites. The online community of men, women, transverse, bi, homosexual, lesbian! It was a strange world out there: Naked or skimpy people in their virtual homes. Doing, planning and enacting the game of sex and love. Not love as it appeared to be purely mechanical sort of things.

I used to wonder more often than not people seemed to be fixated on sex, leaving everything behind. It has acquired a sort of status symbol. People posting their new acts, some new experiments before public. How come a private life has become public act or it is sheer exhibitionism from hindsight. Even out of this they get satisfaction! Strange world is it, having the potentiality of threatening the human space and mind.

But for me, it was all, everything, even if for the time being. It was present presence but this present being seemed to be in suspended animation mode, neither leading to future nor leaving any legacy. A thing or being in itself that has no being. The problem is, I seemed to be generalizing, that we have been conditioned to one gender and fixed sexual choice. That is why one feels as if he or she were doing something wrong.

But the question remains unresolved. If it is personal choice, how could be it wrong when the right and wrong is based on the shifting lines, on the blurring of boundaries, crumbling of the premises and shaking of the grounds on matrix of exigencies and convenience!

3

Curves and crevices! Life seemed to be veering around these existential and non-existential entities, metaphorically and literally as well. At every curves and turns life takes new turn and new journey. New scenes and seer! Observer and observed! Ups and down, twirls and twists. These are breathtaking some time, while gasping for breaths other time. This moment bringing the being on top of the world, other one would be plunging right into the precipice and crevices. Light: lighted darkness, enlightened.

Every curves and crevices give into to new ones. Just like that of flesh! Taken over by the life curves and crevices, bitten and bruised, frayed and fried in the heat, dust and cold of life! Then seeking the solace and succor in another sort of curves and crevices! Length and size, broad shoulder and cupped beauty!

Sometimes it looks like as if life is nothing but the curves and precipice. Either one is going into it or going out: but they are the constant factor. Crevices and recipes literally as well as metaphorically! But they are what life is! So it seems we have made them as what they are curves and precipice as such. Form inside to outside curves and crevices; from outside to inside its there. Everywhere: here there. In fact life itself seems to be the curves and crevices! Is it logical fallacy of moderns or illogical one, I was confused

If so, be it so. Then why not be the curves and crevices himself or herself. A change without physical change but, feel like or be like seems to be mating at one point-when there is no barrier of gender, sex and any sort of difference of caste creed or religion. There is perfect harmony of one with all.: A sort of liberation, Fee in every respect. Guilt is there, regret, self loathing is there: sometimes or may be for all time to come. Depends you know how do you view. If your ego is gone, self is freed from any limitations and boundaries. Then you are free to float over the whole universe. Have all of them or have them in all, that appeared to be big question!

The latter realization dawned soon. After having them all! Now have them all like Kajal did or I was about to redo. After scaling scores of curves and crevices: Now be the curves and crevices. Its there, it has been right inside me but ego failed to see it. When ego gone, name, place, space time, gender and benders gone: it is there inside me, what if only on ideational level!

But soon it would threaten to become a reality while visiting the same sex massage parlors. It was an evening like a night that never going to end as if! Inside and outside appearing to have become one with intersecting each other! All barriers, limitation and conditions gone, even if all were there! It was perhaps because the ego was forsaken in the intoxication of dark passion. Free floating being: from this to that. All possible role plays! In that process, even if at thoughts and ideational level, the tension and pain got intensified. With pleasure in all varieties and versions verging on the perversion! It does not matter: everything is fair and fair in this free floating being. I felt like having massage, that too from -same sex massage.

The bi curiosity could not be denied.. After payment I was ushered into massage room by stud looking tribal folk. After changing into a piece of see through clothes or at best no…. on my stomach, head down and legs apart. He was massaging from behind. When to the valley and crevices, I would squirm and moan like Kajal used to do.

'Comfortable, massager asked. Not liked or what?

'No..like that…I liked.

He would start the massage. Slowly, gently and the more deftly but his all pulls and pressures seemed to be ending to the crevice, valley and the well. As if the destination of his fingers journey from the toes to camel toes. I would eye him from the corner of eyes. He appeared like Stud type, supple and hard! An aroused was he like me. Up and down. My whole body would feeling his fingers, like woman. I would have been responding otherwise he would not have started fingering. A muffled moan was emanating.

Then the massager would come beside me. I was lying on my tummy, legs spread. Now he would start massaging back, shoulder and waist and not forgetting to touching the valley and beyond. Then he would start rubbing his thong to my face in synchronized manner. He was fully aroused. Each time his thong and fingers touched he kept on saying:--oh yo got beautiful body..its very good, not seen like you. One time I felt like taking into it like Kajal used to do. And he did not fail to notice me tangoing him.

'Rest would be at your home I did what officially allowed, he abruptly halted and said gasping for breath.

I thought he was kidding. I did not imagine he would turn at my home, so enamored he seemed to have become of me. And that night set the new beginning: from bi to gay, lesbian, bi and transverse as well. Questioning and IA would come later on.

4

The masseur-his name was Tanny- came like a minor wave but soon it would turn out to be an ocean of new life. New experience and feelings- a sort of new birth seemed to have dawned.He would carved a female and beloved in me. He would have changed me into his lady love with band of magic.

-'Oh you are great marvelous. i could not control myself from barging at your place at night. Tanny said while sitting on sofa. Sorry… I hope not disturbed you.

'Not at all. I assured him while looking at him from to face to bottom. He was looking handsome, darkly tanned and handsome. A guy would also agree. Had Kajal not deserted, she would have fallen for him- tall, good face and stud type. With muscles and toned body. Then all of sudden Iwould embarrassed at such thoughts. He noticed my blush.

'I have seen hundreds of men and woman but not like you, Tanny said to me sitting beside me on sofa.. A manly perfume poked a beloved in me. I No Idea why I started feeling like Kajal- my ex live in partner. As if she had entered me despite having deserted me for long!

'No joking… serious…….really, he said while taking me in his arms like her lovers used to do. You are great babe I love you. He started kissing and his tongue inside me. I just left myself at his beck and call. Then he would start kissing vehemently down to neck and below. I did not feel like protesting. In fact I was enjoying. And then he would undressing me and self as well. When finished he said: let me me free you from hairs. And he put a lotion that he always kept with him being masseur.

When he showed me in mirror hugging from behind and fingering with one hand and patting rather squeezing my chest and nipples like guy one. Then I did as she used to do with her lovers. He started licking everywhere as her lover used to do.

Thus was I baptized into new gender: female in male body? Fist time noticed my nipples like sixteen years as he pointed.

'Oh I you are virgin, he said with unbound joy. He was cleaning and shaving my new found asset. It was given virgin like treatment. It was new experience and a new being and gender was taking shape. The original one was giving in happily to female gender. But I had not an inkling then that I would be trapped in no gender's land.

The new born and sixteen year gal in me would be taking its shape. Tanny had seeded me with new gender. He had become my lover and I his beloved. Oh really its great experience. Be receptive to everything: take it, this that and all. Life is lover and we are beloved in one sense or in many sense depending upon ones IQ and EQ. It was penetrating, giving pleasure in pain!

Read or heard somewhere: there are some sects in some cultures-religions invoking lover and beloved relationship with god and goddess. There are some sects that seek to attain liberation through sex and intoxicants. When one is intoxicated with wine or woman he or she loses, her or his ego, being, and all the limitations and barriers melt away like dew drops. After repeated rituals and orgy of wine and sex, the same type of consciousness and state of forgetfulness of ego and being is sought to attain without it.

The Feeling was beyond any experience! I had left my gender taking refuge in that of other. Without being burdened by that of others. But the danger of being stuck up in others gender or no gender land or realm would be there.

To die in one's gender is better than to live in others as it would be death of both gender. This I realized when found stuck in no gender land: Transverse. Before reaching at the stage of questioning, my answer sheet would become invalid for any question or answer!

5

The new found Freedom had become fetter. The pleasure pain and all the dishes that were so delicious had started appearing gut wrenching. The role playshad had to the frigidity and impotency. I could not fit into any role. The swirling changes in role plays had rendered the self unfit for any further role change. For that matter no role was giving rise to any passion. It was just another act. That is what it is. Like hunger, thirst or any urge to possess.

But it had acquired a status of its own. A life style, statement of being free and high. I had gone to meet Sarah and Jeb to explore my being to be free and have meaning in life. But here I got deep in stuck up staccato!

Perhaps to one role-gay. Nobody could bargain for such obsession that would be more of the compulsion rather. A ping pong of gender, rather distortion or perversion of gender! Violation of nature and its order! But since it was volition of my choice, how did it matter. As my being is also part of nature. So far so good, but why this pang for normality, why craving for normal things!

'What's wrong with it? Jeb interjected. When gay and lesbian has been termed normal, there should not be any doubt about

-'For what shake you are having doubt Maan, Sarah cooed to me.

'But why does it seem as if something wrong has happened, feeling of being wrong, a sort of guilt and regret'… I said.

'Its your individual problem, I think. Jeb concluded. And Sarah went to kitchen to fetch something surprising for us.

'But I was saying that this role plays of LGBTQIA is threat to our culture, not only culture but very being, I tried to pick up the matter where it had been left.

'How could it be so, Jeb said. No idea.

'Look at me. For example it has rendered me incapable and rather incapacitated for any normal relations. Unable to do anything. Even I lost my gender but not acquired the role of any, no desire. In fact, very desire has left me. Even if it comes for some time, it goes away the moment it hits me.

'Oh great Maan! You have attained Moksha or liberation a sort of, Sarah rather said Jokingly.

'It can be said in one respect. But it is out of helplessness. Its by default… my inability., I opened my heart without any hesitation. Its different from desire less state that follows liberation or Moksha . In that situation desires fail to pep up, here desire do come, that in wholesale but its inability to be fruitful that rile the situation.

'But that's your problem, both expressed their sentiment at the same time.

Jeb and Sarah both were not getting what I was trying to point out. How could they? They had not undergone the ordeal suffered by me. Even though they also seemed to have stuck to their opposite genders respectively, butthey seemed to be happy in that. Ignorance could be bliss sometimes, now I would come to realize it.

It was of course my problem. But does individual matter arise in vacuum? Has not it linkage with the society? The LGBTQ has come to fore as movement to give right and respectability to the sexually deprived and underprivileged. It is for their empowerment, not for life style!

The doorbell rang. Sarah went to receive the unexpected guest. There enteredMr and MrsKohli.

'We were discussing with MrMaan the LGBTQ matter, Jeb briefed him about our discussion.

But for me it seemed to have lost any interest. Not only this, I seemed to have lost interest in everything. Even very life seemed to be meaningless. The throbbing pain of guilt and regret was not leaving me wherever I used to go or do whatever used do. As if I had done something wrong and it was sapping all passion and energy for life.

'What's wrong with it, MrKohli said taking the cup form MrsKohli whom Sarah had asked to pass. If one gets meaning in life, some enjoyment and interest in every day routine life…. I don't find any wrong in it.."

'That's what I was saying, Sarah said looking at me. Jeb did not like it.

'what do you think MrsKohli, Jeb said trying to get MrKohli's love through his partner.

'You are right Jeb, MrsKohli said.

'But Jeb has not said anything, MrKohli teased his partner.

Now, it was becoming difficult to stay put there. A sense of alienation and loneliness had gripped my whole being. Their talks and pointless interjections would appear to be trite and boring.

'Some important work, I said to Jeb. I have to go. Please excuse…

The gut wrenching feeling, a sort of nausea would continue to pinch. I thought it would subside in open air. Outside it was beautiful evening. People were returning from offices .Heavy rush was on the road and in the markets. A nerve soothing wind was blowing. The Sun was hurrying forth on to horizon, and the silhouettes of skyscrapers and tall buildings were getting larger.

But I was feeling as if something wrong had happened and still happening. It was as if I had done something wrong for which I won't forgive myself. Despite rationalizing this as morality and right and wrong, being conditioned by society, the guilt and repentance were putting me down.

Moreover, I was finding myself stuck in no gender realm. I would be neither able to keep normal relations, nor to any of the roles. A sort of frigidity and impotency seemed to grip me.. Desires and jest for life seemed to have deserted.

I was passing through South Avenue marketplace. I heard someone calling my name from behind. When I turned back , it was Prof Waru, my long lost friend.

We went to nearby restaurant to celebrate our chance re-union over coffee and cutlet. And we would be back to our old game and period, reliving them virtually!

6

Prof Waru was teacher of robotic science having done many pioneer works in the field of Artificial Intelligence. He was considered the top ranking researcher in robotics in general and AI in particular. But he had developed immoral and inhuman penchant for replacing humans with humanoid, and his angle of research to supplant rather supplement the human being, had earned him the defame and isolation that he did not bargain for.

He could not complete his research. That was the forgone conclusion when he had started the work on this inhuman rather immoral subject. Even then we used to differ in many respects in this regard. The main point of difference was: he had more faith and hope on robot decked with IA than humans. He believed that human should pave way for robot with IA as humans have been unable to go beyond instincts, emotions and the cluttered mind.

I would not share Waru's unfounded faith and optimism in robots decked with AI. When human beings themselves have utilized only tiny corpus of vast potentiality of mind and intelligence, how could robot and artificial intelligence would go beyond it. When humans themselves are hurtling between the borderline of tribalism and modernity, this confusion and limitation would percolate to it. Related with it is the twofold problem of human existence: things and events occur in their own ways guided as they are with their own cause and effect dynamics. For this reason, it is difficult to predict and anticipate the effect and turn of events.

In addition humans are limited by the worldly, existential and mental and bodily constraints. This would put robot with AI on same footings with human. With all follies and limitations. But one disadvantage: the robot with AI would be unable to tap dynamics of intelligence. Intelligence with its infinity need entity like mind to find manifestation which robot would be unable to tap. Even if simulated with artificial mind. Intelligence like Soul or electricity or energy need a medium to manifest itself—a medium that facilitates it to be, a sort of originary and intrinsic to the entity or the being.

'You don't see Maan, Prof Waru would say, the smart robot fitted with AI is as good as any human. I would rather say better off than us in more than in one respect. No emotions and instinctual and bodily and mind limitations. Rational …..

'But its hypothetical assumption about it, I used to say usually. When human has not gone beyond borderline of modernity and tribalism, how robot and AI could be rational and decision making entity. It could make decision or do as what would be fed on not beyond.

'But……

-On Prof just let me finish, I would say. When an unprecedented, unexpected and unanticipated events or situation arises that usually happen in the life, human intelligence and mind have been just ineffective in many respect. It has not yet led to existential growth of beings. Despite enormous and mindboggling growth and development we humans are unable to know the turn of events, except in probability. When human has been unable to negotiate this, how could robot and AI crafted by him or her could do so. In fact, IA and robot could act worse in such situations, the law of probability notwithstanding. Moreover….

'So you are against AI, he would argue.

'Not really. It's a sort of precaution. Humans existentially have remained same and whatever is mooted, conceived or atifacted or crafted by them would reflect in that. For example the culture that has developed over the ages till today betrays all tribal and pre-modern traits.

-For example? Waru sought. His whole defense line seemed to have been challenged.

-Race, caste, kinship, hostility to other, selfishness, Us vs them, honor killing, promiscuousness. We are still seem to be stuck up in rather a sort of childhood of existential growth. Same anger and jealousy, rivalry and hostility, selfishness, out to bay for blood for other for their own kinsmen, caste, race, language and religions. We are living in layers of hostility for others and there endless number of division and otherness points, starting with race, caste clan, tribe, religion.

Other is hell, said Prof Sinha, while entering our discussion. He was Professor of Logic at local college.

'That is what has been made out to be by the culture and civilization developed so far. Other is not hell but a sort of bliss through which life unfolds itself. Only condition is that you do not consider them as other but extension of self. But look what has been made out to be. All humans seem to be herding in their respective enclosures of stark otherness,-race, caste, color, creed, religion, ethnicity, language, nationality. What is unfortunate that they bury their being and identity in such enclosures by default.

-You are digressing from subject, said Prof Waru. It would be breakthrough in technology and human would be at complete rest and enjoyment of desires and indulgences. The leisure and pleasure that he would avail would be unprecedented in whole civilization….

-But it would make the humans a dumb and mindless lazy creature… whom the very robot decked with AI invented by humans would ultimately devour, if not literally then metaphorically like Franksteinian Monster. With all works and sense stimuli and desires and their fulfillments outsourced to smart robot, the mind would be dumb entity floating in vast immanence! Its all faculties would in due course of time be atrophied as per law of nature. An organ or biological entity gets atrophied when not in use for a certain period. Over few generations we as specie might get extinct…

--Very true Mr. Maan, Prof Sinha agreed to the ire of Prof Waru. But I did not know he would loose control of himself and instead of blasting us would just take leave of us. It is typical response of his type of intellectuals and research scientists: take it or leave it. They want their hypothesis and assumptions proven without having proved them and hence must be accepted . even If one does not agree with it.

I am not against the AI, for that matter no right thinking could be ever be. But the increasing gaping divide between the technological breakthroughs and human beings remaining in its infancy of existential growth and being, is resulting into the coconut fruit- in- monkey- hand syndrome-monkey using it like ticking bomb. While technological growth is happening in leaps and bounds, the humans have remained stuck up in the pre-modern mode. The more they refuses to accept their existential stagnation coated with all modern claptraps, the gap is getting nor critical with technology leaping exponentially.

I knew Waru had some other goose to geek over. Whatever I would gather from him that he was nursing secret desire of ruling over the country through robots, IA and humanoid. His father was a failed politician hailing from Northeastern part of the country. And he was the failed scientist00. Despite it he was working in very systematic way on this project. He had devised three pronged strategy to reach his goal: Family, community and society. Then he was working on family. He had devised a family of robots-Mother, father and son and daughter.

He was living in the virtual world. It is something like an instance happened to a sage. one day He would see in dream that he was a bat. And he could not be assured which was real: he or bat. He thought he is bat as he had been dreaming about being a human!

The future world replacing humans with humanoid and smart robot with AI: it was dangerous ambition of Waru. He had been working in systematic and planned way in this direction. Even if it was a sort of   chimera, a paper boat out to sink. Never the less, he would be working on the three stages of his dangerous project: family, community and Society.

From hindsight he could not be faulted for this dangerous and immoral maneuverings than the technology and politics of technology. The technological strides that have been hyped or being hyped is the spoiler perhaps. If seen from right perspective, there has not been any major breakthrough lateral invention other than computer and internet. The hype of artificial intelligence and digital revolution is but its horizontal growth or extension. As is the wont of we modern aki postmodern or post-postmodern! The technological extension and lateral development is being given gobbling makeovers of hypes and hoopla!

7

The other day Prof Waru called me. He wanted to solve a

problem or suggest some way out from that he seemed to be stuck up with. The problem: his family project of robotics with AI had been stuck up in emotions and family bonding.

'Well Maan, Prof Waru opened his heart the moment I settled to his high tech hospitality, imploring with anguished diffidence. Can you help me out….?

'I told you earlier as well…it is bound to fail….

'Please don't bat for morality and ethics, he quipped with sarcasm unbound.

'But this is against nature…a sort of moral impropriety against humanity, I said.

'Well, I have not called you for preaching but helping me out…. Not ..you know…, he said rather arrogantly.

'OK then give me permission to take your leave. I hit back with resolve to leave his house cum lab.

'Oh sorry, Prof said putting his right hand on my shoulder. You are the only person that I value very much. He paused for a minute; I know it is going to fail. But for sake of trying and development of science and technology … there is nothing wrong in trying it..

- But tell me how could you put emotion in intelligent robot, I said.

-just as IQ is put through chip , it would be done in the case of EQ and it will be done, he said

-Sir..Sir..how cold it be done when emotions are dependent variable on stimulus. Even a number of stimulus is simulated, how could it negotiate when unanticipated and unprecedented things happen, that usually do. In addition spontaneity and individuality will be missing.

'But chip can be fitted regarding spontaneity…

'How? When one does not know what situation would develop or exactly in what way and how things would unfold. When humans have been unable to know, till now, as to what would happen in next moment, how it would simulate it, I said. After..

'Law of probability, multiple possibilities node can be added, he put his point very feebly knowing he is standing sticky ground.

-But Sir, Humans are very unpredictable because the life situations and events are like that. No doubt, decision making can be put into robot through AI. The experience and its reaction can be fed into decision making, but nature and things in life generally do not repeat and replicate themselves. How could robot take decision of thing that have not taken place yet. How could be it fed in robot that yet to happen and decision yet to make. How robot would negotiate that situations?

'Well Maan, Prof Waru said, these could be synergized with basic principal and theory of decision making and anticipation..

'All said and done, but tell me how would you deal with love, sex, filial feelings, bonding and mutual love

'You better know this could be also done with fitting microchip of love, sex, etcetera …..

'Best of luck Prof Saheb! Saying I took his permission to leave. But he asked me to stay for the drinks.

'But you know I don't drink, I said.

'oh sorry. Then at least give me company—you take soft drink…, he said. He opened his bar chest and fetched one bottle of imported wine and a cold drink for me.

He appeared to be very lonely. There are two places where one usually feels lonely-top and bottom. But I was not sure Prof Waru belonged to which one. But I was sure that he was lonely. After a couple of pegs, he would start opening up.

-Maan....Maan you are great. You give frank opinion. But where was humanity and morality when my father was hunted like hare. I was not allowed to finish my research work. I could get job in any university. Even the foreign universities have blacklisted me..... what was my fault? I was working on robotic project to create a being similar rather better than of humans... tell me what is wrong with it...

I nodded in affirmation. It is futile to argue with a drunk. More so to a person intoxicated with revenge and diabolical intention.

'Do you know what I would do, Prof Waru was bragging. I would make a society of smart robots with AI and it would replace the human society one day. First I would infiltrate the power node of society and supplant the politicians and bureaucrats with my smart robots , programmed with wherewithal to take over the whole system. After supplanting the ruling elites of powerful countries, I would rule over the world. And slowly but steadily humans would be replaced with smart robot.

His face would be blurred with malice and diabolical shades and lines. I could not help but laugh inwardly sometime, other time just stealing a look into his red blurred eyes. His grudge against humanity would be contorting his face beyond recognition. When he lost consciousness ,I just sneaked away from his home. It was more a technical ghetto than a home. A feeling would overcome me as of someone should bang his head against wall.

8

I was on the way to home. I was feeling very depressed: About nothing specific. As if something grave would have happened. But then I would discard them as being mere thoughts having no substance, as they have no foundation. Human mind and thoughts are unfathomable. They seem to be endless pit of nothingness: despite crowded with thoughts and its effect, but in reality they seem nothing but so crowded, fleeting and immanent they are!

But life seemed to be having something more for me.

When I reached home, it was almost afternoon. But an aura like death in the afternoon seemed to be wafting. Why? It would soon become clear. Heckles were raised a bit when massager did no not open door for quite some time. When the massager opened the door, he would be in cross dress of a girl. I was unable to ascertain whether undressing and getting dressed. He greeted as if not welcome this time, as if her/his privacy had been intruded, as if she were the owner of the house!.

A cacophony of muffled voices were emanating from anteroom. What was going, I was wondering. Moaning, cooing, fast and cascading breath were givng exciting cover to this mystery. When I preened into it, it seemed to be moving away from ante room to balcony n back to room. It might be echo.

But when I zeroed down I found the massager that had become guy was enjoying with a black stud guy. A strange world seemed to be unfolding: fluid identity and gender. No barrier and limitations were there. One could be what wanted: a gal, guy, transgender, bi, hetro and 3s, 4s and group. Innocence and ignorance is bliss, so is having no physical and mental boundaries we seems to have entangled our being, life and its roles.

Role, roll: Unroll and loll. Folding, unfolding, and expanding like limitless sky. The Self and the body encasing it seemed to be permeable and mixing with whole. No self or the body, only process it appeared. The only limiting and binding thing would be: to desire, to be, the wish and impatience for wish fulfillment It would be only thing seemed to be putting back to there from where being feels free.

But when I tried to enter the limitless vast world of pleasure, the massager having become lady would rebuff. He was engrossed with the asset of black guy. He now as she was lolling the assets like prized catch with the whorish dexterity. The scene and seer were so gawking beyond any precedent. The kick was so powerful that even I would like becoming like she and partaking the ultimate fantasy.

'Go away, you would scare my lover, said the massager who was role playing of a lady. They were in 69 formations. The basic instinct show would go on. The primordial urge would remain so: now elevated to the gateway to the carnal and banal freedom. They were deep into each other. And I would feel the intruder, but they did not seem to be intruded. The show was going on. The show must go on. I too started, even on only by seeing them, being she with love unbound. Their very presence seemed to be opening the floodgates of unlimited love and limitless passion and pleasure.

But soon I would be grounded to the hard reality. Despite shifting from one gender to another, changing sexual orientation at the drop of hat. It was so exciting rather exhilarating/ oh God! It was like heaven in the form of flesh and flesh taking unchartered ground of happiness and excitement. But in that tango my real gender would got hanged. Or rather it would be lost in the no gender land of fluid gender. I must have gone mad. Better check out with psychiatrist.

After leaving the modern subpoena, I rather went for the suicidal and hysterical drive. I did not remember exactly how long. But when returned, he who had become she had again become a transverse. One white guy had also joined. With brown and yellow and mixed already in tow! It was the perfect medley of world, an international potpourri.

Knock…knock…bang….. bang. But I seemed to be odd number there when the coupling, tripling and four squaring were being played out.

'Go away, yelled the massager.

It was my home, my place and everything mine. And then look at how this guy was behaving! I took the help of some of my neighbors and colony security personnel. And they along with massager were evicted right there.

These left me dejected and just aghast at the turn things had taken place. Rather dumbstruck I rushed to Sarah place. But Sarah was nursing her unsatisfied sexuality as Jeb having become she or homosexual had gone for rendezvous with his partner. Seeing me at this moment when she was arranging a party of all sort of roles to be enacted, she would all gaga for. Hugging and doing all sort of things that other were doing group, she started warming me up.

Sarah-epitome of sexual freedom and liberation would suggest the multiple mode, roles and partners and genders blast. She wanted to re-do the reverse order: she, me, and her two equally voluptuous friends. Sarah was excited to the hilt, fired with endless round of passion. But the center, that was me was unable to hold periphery of Sarah and her two friends of obscure gender.

The center not sure of its gender and role would be just on the margin when periphery was on top. This mismatch would lead to a lot of discord. Periphery after collapsing of center would be trying to be the center apart from being a periphery. But the periphery trying to be center as well when center was itself in quandary: and at last would suffer from indeterminate gender.

Afterward there would be the crumbling of center and periphery both: Sarah was planning to arrange swing party. And I ? Perhaps to check out with any nearby psychiatrist!

PART
2

1
FREEDOM OR FETTER

Maan was thinking that he had gone mad. He was sure he had gone nuts. The abnormality had seemingly crept into his mind and become a recurring narrative of his personae. Sometimes he would feel at the top of world, while other moment he was sinking deep in morass and depression. Nothing seemed to be going right and everything had gone bad, as if.

Maan was fed up with modern life and it's shifting life styles, freewheeling and free dealing. He was bored to the death. There would be no way out from this. No new alternative was visible that would keep him going on in life. He could not find the meaning and purpose for living. He was fed up with his life and the banal routine of daily life.

In the morning he would wake up with tons of guilt and repentance. A sort of self-loathing and self-beatings would follow. To blunt this or submerge these pricking conscience pangs, Maan would again reek in this flesh hunting and seeking pleasure in multiples. This, that and everything that would give pleasure to him. But instead he was getting more pain in bargain.

He had staked his life on these evanescent things. He had invested everything on these things. He had no other resource he could fall back on when tides were pretty low. He had thought these things were all that mattered in the life. But when these had become meaningless, he could not bargain for more. He was in the typical situation that moderns usually find themselves. The fallacy of pleasure usually leads to more pain and inner conflict. The beings of modern are left to fend for themselves in the vast chaotic immanence without any oars of morality, conscience and transcendence. Wisdom and knowledge has been discarded as cog in the freewheeling and free dealings of life.

He seemed to have reached at precipice of life! He could not go back as he had reached the cliff hanger by travelling of that route of life. There was no way ahead. He was completely at loss with him. What to do with life. In that state of mind, Maan took an appointment with physiatrist, Jaan Daruwala.

After many sessions stretching over to months, the seasoned psychiatrist diagnosed: You are okay but you are required to do two things: get married and cultivate some hobbies. You need to have meaningful relations and engagements.

Afterwards, Maan literally got some meaning and zeal for life. His new mission in life would become:how to get married as soon as possible. He would start renewing his lost relations and contacts. He would put ads in the newspaper and other media and marriage portals.

But actually Maan was in search of a simple bride for him. A house wife type : if she would be from village and poor family, that was his first preference. For this reason he would hit out the rural areas. He would visit his cousin, Subhash native place on India-Nepal border. His cousin would talk about a child widow in early 20 whose beauty had crossed over the border!

Next morning Maan would set out for her village along with his cousin. They reached there in the afternoon. The village was still and peaceful. It appeared as if it had become one with afternoon. The green fields and ponds seemed to be dozing in the silence of afternoon. The mother of the girl would greet Maan and his cousin with usual village hospitality. The cot with neat bed sheet was laid in the courtyard of her house. The lassi, sharbat and rural snack of roasted cereals would follow.

Then child widow came with tray of lassie in her hand. Maan saw a tall girl with broad shoulder and full bosom. Anyone could fall in love with her at first sight. The whitish complexion was glowing with pink of health. Maan at once told her mother that she was acceptable to him. At this, the girl, Ugia dashed down to adjacent room blushing. Her mother commented the girl was getting nervous.

Maan had found Ugia physically attractive and beautiful. It had aroused passion in him. That made him to say yes to her. In an arranged marriage of this sort, one is expected to decide live with girl for whole life. And one has to decide in few days or hours in some cases. That is very challenging for both girl and boy. Hence the first thing that is put premium over other is physical attractiveness and sexuality. Such marriages start with body and sexual attractiveness. From body it goes to mind and becoming true union of two beings. It is said that for this reason the arranged marriages are more successful than love marriage where the trend is reverse: from heart to body. As heart is very fluid and uncertain it gets strayed in reaching the body level.

Now Maan was marveling at the uniqueness of the arranged marriage. What a stark changeover he was witnessing within his own self. Earlier he would abhor the arranged marriage and traditions and dos and don'ts. After getting his finger burnt in the live-in relationship with Kajal, he was expected to find the resting place or feeling of grounding or home coming. But Maan could not find any of such opportunity of reveries as the mother of bride wanted to finish marriage ceremony as soon as possible.

Actually the bride, Ugia's mother had to bear many difficulties and a sort of social ostracism . The widow marriage was still a taboo in that part of the world! She wanted her child widow daughter marriage at any cost. Ugia had been married when she did not know what marriage is! It was typical insecurity of parents of daughter arising out of huge sum of money to be given in the dowry for the marriage. This fear forced them to relent to the child marriage of Ugia! Poor child! She got married in the age when she was below 10 and became widow within two years!

Maan had agreed to accept her hand. And her mother wanted to marry her as soon as possible. Within few days, the marriage ceremony was arranged in the nearby town, not in village as they were against widow remarriage. And Ugia was sent along with Maan very next week.

Things and events happened suddenly. Maan was at odd with new reality of his married life. That day was the first night of marriage, the SuhagRaat! And he was just sitting bewildered in the side room. Ugia, his bride was awaiting him, made up in bridal make up, with red bridal dress. She was blushing and blushing. She would start feeling her breath choked with excitement. How many times she had fantasized about this night, she was unable to remember. It had been only thing she had been living for, up till now! But why he is not coming, she was getting anxious and nervous.

It was the first wedlock night! SuhagRaat! And Maan entered the nuptial dangeon with forebodings and anxiety of a homosexual. He knew he would be unable to consummate his nuptial responsibility. Still he went there, mustering all his courage and summoning his strayed virility! He had nothing to offer except his failed sexuality!

Ugia! Poor child widow! Remarried but still would be feeling and reeling under apparition of the widowhood! Earlier she was declared widow with attendant social and personal stigma! Now she was declared married but another sort of widowhood had started clouding her thoughts!

Never minding the strange turns and twirls of life, Maan and Ugia would start their life afresh. No question there would be about the past, any regret, any ifs and buts. Whatever life would be giving they would accept. Its routine, ups and downs of the daily life with all hustle and bustle would be on offer. They would take it as it was. They would be living: without any hangs up, any attitude. No prejudice that they this should be like and that should not have done that way or happened this way. It should happen now or never.

Not giving in to any desire, fancy and cravings of all sorts, they would keep on going in their new life. But Ugia was filled up with all sorts of cravings and desires! She was feeling like trapped in the unending churning of desires and craving for unrequited love and sex. She would feel like a fish remained thirsty amid the bubbling water of ocean!

But what was available in natural way (sahajrup se)both husband partner would be living that. No strivings, no cribbing for extra masti and some kick. They would live on like a good grihasth, trying to spend the ideal married life.

But one day everything would change. History would repeat itself but with its renewed intensity and ferocity of unknown and unexpected.

1

One day, it was not an ordinary day! It was Ugia birth day. Maan had arranged small dinner at his home. And Prof Waru came in to their surprise. Like uninvited but not unwanted !at least for pretty Ugia! They have forgotten to invite him. Because he was just not the type for the small gathering they had worked out.

He had heard from some common friend about Ugia birth day. He just barged into, with carload of expensive gifts. Ugia had just fallen for him. She was hugging him more than once. Maan doubted they had something more when they had gone to anteroom on some pretext. And she would be taking care of him more than any guest. She had turned a sort of possessive to the extent raising heckles and eyebrows.

When all guests were gone, Prof Waru would reveal his magical game plan. He was ahighly ambitious man having not so secret desire to rule over the world through his Intelligently Smart robot! One day he wanted to see this happening in this life itself. And Maan did not invite him for party. He had not invited even on his wedding and nor informed about. He got so enraged and his vindictive ego so hurt that he was burning with his desire to pay in equated coin. In fact his incensed ego had got so touchy that he thought anything would justify it.

But when he saw Ugia and her desperate eyes! Green eyes embezzled with a light parrot shades of green! His whole devious senses would get ignited with fire. She was not only holding her eyes but inviting Prof Waru to take her to ultimate desire. When they hugged, her body seemed to be blipping 'Take me away... oh baby ..., She also told her in ears: Come after sometime to anteroom. And there her unrequited desire, love and marriage would be consummated in that few minutes. She felt as if that night was her real *SuhagRaat* or Wedlock night!

'Maan! Permit me to use Ugia look alike for a project, said Prof Waru throwing his devious dice

'what and which project, Maan and Sugia said at the same time. They were just taken back his proposal.

'but it could be misused.. its unethical, Maan said.

'let it be like that, Ugia said. What's wrong in it. I just want to see how robot looks like me.

--o Waru ..doit..i just want to from see it …said Ugia hugging him once more.

The reality behind this façade would start unraveling soon. Actually Waru had fallen for his friends partner the moment he saw her for the very first time. She had heard about her titillating beauty from many. It was his lust for his friend's partner that made him to devise such devious plan. And Maan despite guessing his game plan could not do much. As Ugia seemed to be more keen to have her lookalike robot or rather clones than any sort of relationship. Lately she seemed to have developed liking for him. More often than not she was with Waru, helping him to make her look alike smart robot.

But Maan would not have thought that Waru would exchange his partner with the cloned one. He just could not have imagined such possibility. But it happened, on the very night when his Ugia 2.0 was ready. And Waru had organized a party on this occasion. On that day Maan repented his decision to give in to his proposal. The way Ugia was acting as if she along with Waru had thrown a party, and he was just a guest. Not she. She was having attitude of hostess.

When Waru unveiled Ugia 2.0, it was just masterstroke. The robot Ugia was just like her. She would be in the same dress-long skirt with short blouse. Same color and design. He had also made same dress for Ugia as well. When both were face to face, it was being difficult to recognize who was the original Ugia and who was cloned one. Such was rather the diabolic finesse of Waru work.

And such brilliantly executed was the game plan that it would be revealed much later on. By that time it would have become too late. But Maan had not an inkling then that Ugia had been exchanged with robot one. And Maan was being cuckolded unknowingly. But Ugia seemed to have done it knowingly and willingly to assert her freedom of conjugal right, denied by his homosexual turned heterosexual husband.. He had challenged Waru to prepare the most powerful robot with AI and all possible innovations. And he would worst that robot and if unable to do so , Maan would support him in his all endeavors.

-Ok buddy! I take your challenge. But allow me to go for honeymoon with my robot partner, he said holding Ugia tight. Maan felt as if he were doing to his Ugia!. But robot Ugia gave a very shy and mischievous smile that was like his one. But mine was with me, he hugged her probingly. She was mine one, Maan would be assured.

2

It is said that man is helpless before nature, world and its forces, and the powers that move it. But Nature could not help one feel helpless unless and until one allowing it to so happen . Nature does not play dice. The all talks of freedom seem to be futile! As Freedom from whom and who avail or not avail freedom! We seem to be seeking freedom from free entity that is free in itself.

The being of a human being is free as is resultant of the infinite series of interplay of cause and effect that Nature has been manifesting through. But it has never played dice. We are free entity in real sense of term, if viewed from soul theory. Otherwise also we are free but bound with thoughts, desires and wishes of one own. I think therefore I don't exist!

We are bounded; it seems, by ourselves, zillions of thoughts and desires with no oars in vast ocean of immanence! That is what life at existential level and life at worldly level is its projection of this conundrum! The scenes of life changes like fast cut movies. The fast changing scenes and scenarios zooming past us and we remain stuck up in the gone by moment and instances or forthcoming one.

The present, the current moments and instances bypass us and it continues till the end, to begin again and again. The moderns have displaced knowledge, Soul and God. And they would creep and crib that conscience no longer pricking, forgetting that it not even ticking, it appears. It seems to be almost dead, or gasping for breath. But the moderns do not care for these perhaps, Maan was thinking.

It seemed to Maan as fetter rather than Freedom. When freedom becomes fetter, man or woman does not know what to do. But it is for those who consider, they are the majority view of minor or the part reality viewed as whole perspective that they are different from themselves, superior from other, form nature, world and its forces and power. When one considers one being has become all, there is no other at existential and spiritual level both. There is no other, the other is own extension-one. If not agreed, then others become hell!

But alas! On existential level we don't have any other viable option. There seems no other choice available either. That time Maan did not know that Brahma has no alternative. Even if his being was situated in the Brahma and in fact he was the Brahma himself. And he would be feeling like liberated.

But this seemed to have come out of the helplessness and utter inability to do anything. Be it like it or that as if he had no grudge. Even though he seemed to be still stuck up in, rather stranded in no gender land, unable to do justice to any gender. Maan but could not be assured of the trick that Ugia and Waru were playing. The robotic Ugia had supplanted the real and he had eloped with real one on honey moon. That Ugia could not enjoy love making and she was unable to make spontaneous love making Maan could not know it. As he was stuck up in no gender realm of being! There was some fleeting feeling that he might be tricked, but would get lost amidst the vast ocean of thoughts and desires.

One day while asserting his lost gender unsuccessfully, he would see a black spot on her private part. That was like star on mount of Venice. It would remove whatever doubt might have arisen. Even it would have arisen, Maan but could not remember. But to alert mind it would have sealed the suspicion. Sometimes he would marvel the change that had enveloped Ugia. She had become docile and homely partner. He was unable to satisfy her, even unable to make sex with her, but she was not complaining. It was strange that it did not give rise to suspicion or some sort of something gone wrong with her.

Maan seemed to have lost his mind. He was stuck up in no

gender realm. He would be busy for nothing in refuting Waru's unfounded faith on smart robots at the cost of humanity. The predicament of having stuck up in no gender land seemed to have robbed him of all the self-esteem and purpose of life. The suicidal feeling followed by nausea and meaninglessness of life was becoming routine matter. It was time to check in with psychiatrist Kim Aahuja.

Maan seemed to be hallucinating : I, the eternal self and eternal friend of Maan, as well as kajal, Sarah, Jeb, and all the world residing in their respective selves, as observer of everything. Me, the body of Maan that I reside like that of Kajal, Sarah, Jeb, Waru and all the people of world body and all busy in enjoying something big, different and rather hilarious one. But are they or for that matter we are enjoying it. Or rather these are using us by enjoying us! It seems perhaps enjoyment in basic instinct and baser precincts the fad of freedom and multiplicity of beings. The choices are there, in unending series of unending chain of choices and life styles that is what life is called today perhaps. Even if Maan was hallucinating, it seemed to be right hallucination!

But more often than not, the unending choices and multiplicity of beings, luring us to be and not to be on the scale of unending reach ability! No sooner than we opt for one, other sweeps us for other and other. It becomes a sort of fetter to do all and be all. If you keep on doing, hopping from one maze of being to other, there is no end. And soon it coils into situation where choices, beings and roles would start guiding and controlling ourselves.

Our real self would become a flotilla on vast ocean of beings and choices. Without any oars of transcendence we seemed to just remain more or like spider hanging by its own web, being preyed upon by time and space that it creates. The toppings of choices, desires, wishes, claptraps of ego, being to be playground of all beings, roles and a hollow barrel with multiple airy nodes would be too alluring to be not caught by these.

But for us moderns, choices and multiple one and enjoying these , availing these have become synonym for the life and its bounty of freedom. We seem to have become the actually choices its self, forgetting the real self and perhaps undermining the reality that it goes beyond these things! Our being seems to be hurtling between one to other choices. And choices like thoughts are imminent and immanent as well, vast and without any limit. But they choose to be what they are and they are what they have been chosen for! Or for that matter what we are. So choices are multiplicity of beings and unending roles of our choice.

But does it matter that prices that one has to pay for such enjoyment of choices, beings and roles are more often than not to be stuck up in no gender land! A realm where one would not be capable of making any further choice and unable to lead healthy life, obsessed with one drive or other or obsessed in one sense enjoyment or other, acting and living under the shadow of many compulsive things!.

For this reason perhaps LGBTQIA as life style would be potential threat to normal heterosexual relations and culture and family and society at the end! Maan's derailed mind seemed to have recovered some lost ground.

Earlier it would be too much of everything. Now it is nothing: A barren land. All freedom has come down to such level that even unable to think about it. All those enjoyments, heavens on earth, pangs of freedom and individualities seem to have become like sweet poison.

3

Maan, on suggestion of Sarah, would go to the psychiatrist, Sejal Baweja- A tall and beautiful lady in late 30s. Slender body with pointed face and hypnotic eyes, radiating very charming rather amorous energy! Well ensconced in the carpeted office and walled with all shades of blue. Seated in black upholstered chair she appeared like ocean unbound when asked, like a ripple in cool and calm water submerging the moment and instance:

'What is problem..Please tell. She said as if she had been waiting to listen since long.

'Well I think I have just gone mad, said . Unable to do routine things…

'If you know, interjecting she said, you are mad. That means you are not mad.

He felt silent for a moment. Then he tried to explain her the problem of his inability to make normal sex. But she would try to hypnotize him. But Maan having strong will would deter her efforts to take control over his being! But she was casting her spell. Fallen already by her beauty, he would got stumped by rather coquettish movements of her body.

'Right madam, its right diagnosis, he replied casting her spell aside. Few years back when he met an accident and he was at hospital, unhurt but very much shocked. When he had said to the doctor that he was in shock, please give me treatment. The Doctor had said if you know you are in shock that means you are not in shock…….

'Ok…o..k..a..y then what, she was not listening. She was dangling one shining bead with one hand. With other she started fondling thighs and beyond. Then she put her milky hand on crouch.

'Then… she said unconsciously, her eyes half closed… its responding babe,,,

'You are normal

'But I am stuck up in no gender land…unable to make normal relations and sex…

'But I suspect, let me check out.'

She virtually raped him and made him do a long session. Even afterward, he failed to convince that had he taken initiative it would have been dud. It was she who made him to do these things. But she could not accept it.

He thought it better to check with some other psychiatrist, particularly male one. He could perhaps better understand his problem. Checking on web, he was able to find a nearby psychiatrist. And he would take appointment for next available slot on priority

Mr Archie Raheja: his new psychiatrist with a long list of foreign degrees and awards. A sort of celebrity doctor, having impressible cliental of celebrities and socialites no body heard about. But good name in the field! He had been recommended by many of friends and known to..

'Good Morning

'So what is your problem, very friendly and charming voice of Mr. Raheja was resounding with ring of deception. The way he spoke as if he were not to discuss some problem but about some soft toy, chocolate and ice cream.

'Unable to make normal sex.., Maan said.

'What about abnormal one? Asked the pot bellied easy going psychiatrist.

'Once tried and got stuck up there…from there could not go anywhere… after some time unable to do anything.

Ok. Tell me details. He said and them ushered him into antechamber. There was dim light there. A couch was there. He made Maan lie down and narrate all that happened recently and not recently.

This narration session went for months. When there seemed to be no end to the unending session, Maan would get restless.

'Sir how long this will go… I have problem of making normal sex.

'With partner or other, he again asked the same question God knows how many times.

'With both, said Maan trying not to be irritated.

'But you said you are getting entangled into homosexual -…

-yeah …but even that no

'But homosexuality no longer is considered as abnormality. So chill if you have become homosexual, he quipped. Then added, female or male?

'Ok, but how could, ignoring his question he shot back, an abnormal thing could be considered as normal. Up till now it was being considered as abnormal. Now it is not so. How and what is this…

'Well! Mr. Maan you have paid me not to give answer to such question. Then he would fall silent and started staring as if I were his prey!

Then all of sudden hugging and kissing like long lost found like lover, he said: you are very handsome and sexy. And started caressing and fondling like lover. Before he would proceed further to test Maan homosexuality, he just ran out from the clinic.

4

After getting disappointed by the modern psychiatrist and psychoanalysis, Maan seemed to have lost even the last refuge. The modern psychology and psychiatry has not grown beyond mind, matter and suppressed of desire. It still seems to have that of nature vs nurture binaries. Taking the roles of the both in factoring of the personality and shaping ones existence, it seems to be drawing a line having hotchpotch of both.

Modern psychology has not yet agreed upon the transcendence and knowledge, as oar to wade through existential conundrum that life is. Even though in its psychoanalysis and another related modern techniques, it provides an understanding and knowledge about one predilection and subjectivity pinning down his personality, and insight and an understanding and acceptance of the problem, it has not given its primacy that it deserves. Soul and existence of God is precluded from any scientific enquiry.

Maan was lost in the conundrum that life is! It was getting darker. He did not feel like going home. It was not home but a place where Ugia used to live. She was no longer that Sugia. But even this fact did not seem to have given any doubt of Ugia having been exchanged.

Then he thought he should visit Jeb and Sarah…but he would again traumatize with his homosexual serenading,…and Sarah..

She would make another part of her 3 s or 4 s rendezvous. He was feeling like homeless despite having home and family. First time perhaps he was getting the feel of being homeless: Homeless despite having home and family.

A strange feeling would seem to have overpowered him! What is but the home when all homes appearing as own or none in particular. When the barrier of a home caves in, it dissolves to become all homes. Not only that there is potentiality of new homes, but one is connected automatically to all the homes having no homes or feeling like having no home despite having the home!

In another sense he or she would become part of universal home or idea of home.   As homes are not made of walls and roofs only, it has relationship and bonding to make it home in the real sense of term. He would wish to forge new relationship and bonding within open sky.   the boundary of homeless home thus would merge with universal home and form there would arise another home.

The crumbling boundaries of homeless would lead to union with universal human home. It would seem to be akin to the breaking of an earthen pot and merging of the sky or empty space within it into or becoming one with the outside sky. It would be one with sky, rather sky itself! It would be nearer to the drunkenness induced forgetfulness of one's ego or its becoming as large as whole world. Maan but could not help to take it with pinch of salt or things going over head or beyond one understanding faculty!

Then all of sudden Maan would remember Prof Waru. More

so his robot patterned on Ugia that Maan believed to be the robot Ugia, but was the real Ugia! This Maan did not know then. Some feeling of something grievously wrong happened would bother him. But he used to discard it as mere a thought and an unfounded suspicion!

Maan shared an unique love and hate relations with Prof Waru: fighting this moment and reconciliation next time. Every time he visited him, Maan used to think that it would be the last visit and he would never come again! But there was something that would attract him!. As if some precious things would have been concealed there!

Prof Waru was very warm-hearted, though crooked and negative in many respects. Even though he was opposed to his most of ideas and acts, still there seemed to be some common ground and bond that used to beckon Maan to his place, more often than not.

Maan decided to visit Prof Waru's home.

5

Maan was on the way to Prof Waru house. He was passing through roads and streets intersecting from the multifarious directions. He would first take the Park avenue Road. Then Ambedkar Road, as there was too much traffic, crossing X Street he came to Highway. The far into maddening rush, the snarling traffic hurtling back and forth like bullock cart, conjugating congestion, the mind renting chaos. Sweltering heat, breath choking pollution. And the sprawling jungle of concrete, steel and glass.

Man would get jittery, at this sort of imposing and a sort of always taxing the life that have evolved in modern times. Then he would get irritated. The trees, the parks, the garden, green stretch seemed to have been overshadowed. A grayish cover would be giving joyless and lifeless artificial look. Or that of his inside color of mood had sprayed the grayish shades all around!

But these are parts of the urban metro life: Life or chaos, mad rush, restlessness. A fierce competitive world we have made, Maan was wondering. World and its forces and manifestations seemed to be going on in its own course, propelled as they are by cause and effect. But for our bloated ego and cravings for more and more of everything, one after one, we often get disillusioned by its apparent reality. That which is real has been put aside in endless number of apparent suppositions perhaps.

In the life and its world, our situation usually becomes like that of a spider. The spider entangled in its own web of desires, multiple beings, all sort of enjoyment and experiences and experiments. It (life) seemed to be left out amidst the vast chaos of imminence that is world. That too without oars of any transcendence or self control—if there is self, then there will be control. Self has been lost to the thoughts and desires and day dreaming, to the multiplicity and all sort of evanescent things. Then what is left out is the freedom of helplessness or no option or too many options!

Maan was having so many options right now. He could go to any number of places: unlimited choices n options. But these multiple options and the engrossing competition among these would render him to nothing as he would be unable to decide any of these. Beyond it his being was taking him to where he would have thought least to go. But going any way! Why, he was unable to understand. Even if Prof was suspected of having done something wrong to Ugia, who was not her usual self, but still he would be preferred to any other. Why? Is he free to choose or these all decided by something or some forces beyond us!

After entering the   Scientist Enclave form Highway, its steel and fiber minarets appeared in the windscreen. Maan remembered: Prof Waru has a family too. A family of robots rather smart ones! Partner and two kids-baby and boy! They deserved some gifts at least, he thought.

Prof Waru could not have mustered enough courage to have family. Marriage and family is big responsibility. He could not bear it, hence he would create or buy a sort of family of robots from grey market. There was to be sub text to this text. He would be rather aggressively ambitious. He was having bizarre sort of attitudinal temperament of making name and fame by hook or crook. He could do anything if it could put to him to fame and big money. The moderns seemed to have too high IQto be fared optimally low in the EQ (Emotional Quotients) perhaps!

The moderns seemed to be rather moving away from herdsman to social being to techno-being. And this techno-being and its hollow multiple beings, without any existential back up and the up gradation since its inceptive journey from the tribalism seemed to have got stranded into the no realm between modernity and pre-modernity. But they would want everything at beck and call of theirs.

With endless number of choices, options and beings to reek in all sort of pleasures, they are seeking more and more. But more they seek the more their cravings for these evanescent things rises. More clutter and accessories we accumulate more isolated we get within. The virtual and digital world has replaced real one. But we crave for the nostalgia of unattainable-all that unfolding and that about to unfold at one go.

Maan vehicle screeched to stop halt at the gate of Prof Waru techno mansion. Prof with his robot family was there. His robot family was looking like as if they would a real one. He could not find any difference. Neither would he recognize Ugia nor his children.

They were in portico, greeting him, with folded hands. With all due formalities and greetings, hugging and all. Amidst all these Maan did not fail to notice the beauty and sex appeal of women robot he claimed to have made. She was attractive and fascinating .One but could not help to fall in love with them.

Waru introduced Ugia as his partner-Max 1 and two sibling Saxes 1-daughter and Gax–son. He also noticed that Prof did not seem to be having love and concern for them. Everything was artificial and artifact like. Even nature and natural things would seem to have been artifact. Or rather distorted and a sort of subversion of everything natural!

After introduction, they would take Maan to his master control room. A sort of semi-cylindrical structure made of potpourri of materials.

-Be comfortable, Prof said to Maan while sitting on the chair seemingly floating. He took a side sofa to rest himself that was also floating. And it would move in the synchronized way with voice going near to person being addressed to sit down. Prof would be on rather a spree to impress him with his tech savvy home.

He pressed the side button of his master control room. The room opened into an alley with 3 D effect, leading to inside. Maxi would appear from nowhere, decked up in black macro and base tops. She would hardly seem to be moving, the elevator like floors beneath her bringing her nearer to them. Then there would be the opening vista like effect, and closed when she would enter the central hall. She was a stunning beauty. No body could say she was robot. But her eyes would resemble that of Ugia perhaps, Maan was wondering!

'Is she same you modeled after my Ugia, asked Maan rather innocuously.

'Not exactly, Prof would-be dodging around. I dismantled that robot as she had developed uncontrollable and mysterious nodes. I could not understand. Moreover, she had started behaving unruly and dangerous....., he stopped abruptly as if hiding something that might have been betrayed.

Maxi came like a smart woman. But she would sit nervously beside him. She was not comfortable in Maan presence. She was fidgeting constantly. She would be reflexively trying rather unfailingly, lengthening her short and skimpy dress. This is really human, she could not be robot. If robot with such accurate human emotions and intelligence, it did not bid well for the future of humanity, Maan was rather surprised!

Maan could not help from feeling suspicious, something fishy! And Waru would not fail to notice it.

'Arrange wine for us, he said to her awkwardly as if his whole deception and conspiracy was about to be revealed. It was obvious he did not want her to be in Maan presence.

Then Prof Waru would go on discussing his new passion: AIS-Artificial Intelligence sex. Maan could not but wink at the way he would mention it! As if it were a sort of breakthrough! Though it is good for those having some sort of sexual deformity, for the same reason it has been added in lexicon of LGTBIAQ. But for fashion and fad and life style option! It would be misused and fraud that that ilk of Waru unknowingly would be perpetrating on the humanity.

'My smart sex robot has become craze, Prof Waru was boasting. You won't feel that its not real. Many customers have emailed and sms-ed about it. I would send one for you…., Prof was not joking.

'Please, Maan said, enough of it… I want to go to bed early as I have an appointment with doctor tomorrow.

'Okay, then go ahead. He did not like it.

He would abruptly and not less awkwardly stand up and say: good night! Rather rudely as if he did not like Maan abruptly leaving his bragging session on the addition of Artificial intelligence to the lexicon of LGBTQIA and its cataclysmic effect on fashion and culture.

6

A horrible night! Rather it was for Maan! At Prof Waru home! Real would not be real, actual not actual in his high tech home. Everything would be illusory: Virtual real and real virtual! Bed was not like bed; room would not be room like. The host would not host and guest not guest! Yet all would be there. But it hardly mattered, at least for him. It would be the same nothingness spread all over. Ugia was not Ugia and his friend Waru not friend. Yet they all were there!

Even sleep was not sleep as it would not be coming near him.

Instead there be gushing volley of the thoughts and the images cascading like a fast cut movies…from cave age, the humans would seem to have landed in the virtual caves of robots and artificial intelligence. It would seem to have completed its circular movement. At the one click everything would be available. Yet everyone would seem to be baying for more and more.

More is no longer more, while less is always lesser. While doer and enjoyer is one proposition but it seems to have been separated. And then, enjoyment is sought in enjoyment and happiness in happiness. As it is bound to be not found as meaning could not be found in the meaning, on this lack and void whole modern seems to be having grounded!

Thanks to the computing, digital age at hind of back to back information age, artificial intelligence and robotics! Humans would seem to have attained a state of being where he is doer without doing and enjoyer of that without doing the act. This would not only upturn the law of karma or cause and effect, but would render the very existence of human species at threat. No work, no use of human intervention as robots with AI would be doing all the works leading to the atrophying of mind and other organs that would remain idle in the long run.

Had the problem limited to it, it would not have that much matter of concern. In the proportion that human minds, intelligence and other organs would get atrophied in due to course of time due non use of these faculties, that of robots, smart robots with IA would get stronger and stronger. When nature plays zero sun game being its principle of never playing dice, how the humans would be getting empowered due to too much dependence on the technology! How could they be immune to such universal natural law? Irrespective of the humans particularly modern and post moderns have demolished all universal and truth by taking out universality and truthiness from these!

And thus there would arise a situation: man would be doer without doing any activities. He or she would be enjoyer without enjoying the life and its trials and travails. The work done would be bereft of any enjoyment and life would be dull, staid and boring routine. The activity and actor duo would be swamped in the artificial cause and effect series giving artificial result. It would be sort of all work no play making John dull and dumb. Human life would be perhaps reduced to hollow hump: a hump without any purpose and substance.

It would not stop even then. The law of karma or cause and effect would be rendered disrupted and a sort of mutilated. And then what would happen is not so difficult to imagine. When the Marxists dice of having upturned the cause and effect by starting with effect or result then undertaking works , have been leading to devastation in all walks of life. Tthis very attack on law or law of karma would throw the baby with bathing water. And ultimately net effect would be just beyond imagination.

Then Maan would remember another friend of Prof Waru. He was an innovative scientist. A sort of zealot type he would be. He was working on extracting energy from anger, violent drive, psychopathic and sociopathic outbursts. He would be working on the criminals and borderline cases of criminality. He would do a lot of experiments and research on the borderline and potential case or people with a lot of anger and sex drive. He was also working reportedly on converting semen and vaginal secretions into energy and electricity. When he would put up the proposal for the research project to a prestigious university, he was shoed away.

But why he would think about these things? Or for that matter why it should be so! He should better sleep as he had an appointment tomorrow with the psychiatrist. Could anyone guess the agony that he was undergoing, Maan was thinking. While world was sleeping, he was awake. It would not be certainly a spiritual sort of things. But the pure earthly ones, he was thinking about his life and Ugia!

The life had become topsy-turvy. And now even sleep would be failing him. While Maan was trying to factor sleep in the sleepless night, usual cat and mouse game would be reenacted. How could sleep grace anyone in Prof Waru's home! His home was violation of everything that would be natural! The day would seem to have been tricked and tweaked into night and the night day. In that melee perhaps his sleep would have been tricked! The whole Warufamily would be following American standard time: sleep during the day time and awake at night.

When Maan got up in the morning, it was 8 o clocks. He had to rush to the Psychiatrist, Dr Sadhana clinic. She had told previous evening: you must report to me at 9 AM sharp,her voice would be ringing like alarm bell.

Maan was wading through canopy of steel, fiber and alloy trees dominating the landscape amidst sparsely grown bonsai trees of all type. When he came out on main road, the matter of normality and abnormality again started debating its nuances in inner races of his mind. The abnormal seems to have become new normal, whereas old normal is being suspected as possible abnormal.

Self-doubt, self-admonition and self-catharsis would start pinning Maan down as the cab snarled down the road leading to DrSadhana clinic. She thought him as normal as he knew, and was aware of what was ailing him. The abnormal does not know about his abnormality. The psychiatrist or for that matter any modern psychiatry is based on this fundamental of making oneself aware what is ailing or lacking. That's all. And exactly it is what transcendence or self knowledge or Aatm-gyan is called in the Indian tradition.

However, there was not something but many things were wrong. But she would say these were okay. He was not sure she was right or he was wrong. But everything was not right as being made out.

-You are late Mr. Maan! The psychiatrist quipped when he entered her room. She seemed to be dressed to kill. Whom he did not know, but prayed silently that he might not be that, praying: not me. But her black macro and more revealing than concealing tops were beckoning him, having stunned his senses completely.

She would notice his eyes glued to her all revealing dress. As if counseling is being consummated between sense and sense objects, and she is the medium, contents and agents – all in one. After all medium is message!

Then her voice started cooing like cuckoo, more hidden then revealed. I tried to know the location of cuckoo in macro n tops. She was c..o..o..i.ng:

'Well..Mr. Maan, she would set the tone of the counseling session, your problem seems to be that of repressed sexuality. Do you understand what does it mean.. I hope I need not explain further…..

'Yea…. A bit …..

'Right. So you have to narrate all of recurring thoughts, fantasies, dreams…frankly without any hesitation and with privacy and security ensured.

'Okay, I said lying down on to adjacent couch.

Thence would start dreams and fantasies sessions. He would recline on a cozy couch in the semi-darkness lit room. She was seated across, up and above a bit near his head stead. Silence… tik …tik …whitish darkness queering the pitch for getting hypnotized. Big eyes…..great breast… ….. the most persistent thoughts ..Desiring sex with everyone. Always wanting to have sex with one and all. And then…….

7

Maan was recreating the fantasies and dreams before Dr Sadhana. He was reclining on couch and she was seated on the upholstered chair beside him. It appeared to be queer situation. The fantasies and dreams that once so fantastic and dreamy sort of things would be now dull and staid. They would appear more like poisonous stuff. How come sugar had become bitter gourd would baffle him. As he was returning from the psychiatrist back to Prof Waru home, the bleak prospect of life and quicksand changes would be baffling him.

Evening almost was dusking when he entered Prof House. A cool and soothing evening had descended on the hanging garden like lawn of the house. But it had lost its beauty and cooling luster amidst the festering sight of the bonsai, artificial trees of steel and fiber. The rows of bonsai plants would be casting its stunted and bonsai silhouette in the fast sliding of evening.

The approaching dusk was morning for Prof home. Presenting an unseen and unheard spectacle, unfolding the bonsai evening getting stuck up in daffiness of artificiality and irrational scheme of things. When one enters his house through arch gate to the path going into two directions, the dwarf jungle of bonsai trees overwhelm ones senses and the very scheme of things of being.

While trudging past escalator like path leading to Waru house, Maan would be feeling a bit relieved after first session with psychiatrist. The artificial grass decked path was bifurcating into two: one going towards the half visible and half invisible main building of his house. The invisible part of his high tech mansion was his work areas where his lab with all bio, non-bio degradable and non-degradable matters and organs were there. This part was in the northern part, separated by swimming pool, lighted by the halogen bulbs.

The central part of his mansion was abode of his partner and his family. This was visible and on its right side was guest house, where he had made Maan stay, was invisible at first glance. But when he would start moving, it became visible with each step! At one glance the house would appear like artificial crescent moon. The suit where he had lodged Maan was once occupied by his ex-smart robotic partner he had dismantled. It was said that robot had started going beyond his control. Thence he had dismantled it.

The smart robot maid named Kini would usher him in his suit. He was yet to decide as to who was more beautiful-Kini or Maxi. The place was too high tech to be called abode for the living. Here it was visible, there it was invisible. The moment one would step out, an escalator would pop up and start taking to destination. With every step, the virtual would be becoming real and the real virtual at same time. It reminded Maan of Maey Sabha of Mahabharata Period. The ancient was being reincarnated or moderns harking back to the ancient! It was being very difficult for

Maan to decide!

Then another robot help would come from nowhere. She too was in very skimpy dress. It appeared as if dress code of Waru house might be skimpy transparent dress. Be it his partner or daughters or assistants or maids or lab attendants - all in same skimpy see through dress. One might mistake it for ultra modern pimp house as well or salon of LGBTQAI! What a striking contrast: while variety is the hallmark of Nature, sickening uniformity seems to be that of moderns!

After having sumptuous intercontinental dinner, Maan would go to bed.   Another maid in the skimpy sexy dress appeared. Throwing a mechanical look, the girl robot would start undressing, to the surprise bordering on vulgarity, to Maan. No sooner than she finished undressing than Waru's partner would barge in, taking position between him and the naked maid, as if shielding him from her spell.

'Kini just go away. I would do the relaxing massage to the guest, said Maxi, Prof Waru partner who was actually Ugia rebooted as Maxi..

Amidst half way of her sensuous and passionate massage would come Prof Waru. He would come with a thud and shrill cries and a laser weapon in his hand. When he was scuffling with his partner Maxi, Maan had had sneaked out from there. Out in open! An Open with openness opening out unendingly and unfolding ad infinitum.

And Maan would look back from the street taking the sharp turn. He saw the razing fire having engulfed Waru mansion. People were rushing out to douse the fire. But not lo and behold, in a moment everything had disappeared in the razing fire!

Two skeletons were found amidst the ashes of Prof Waru high tech mansion. When Maan rushed to his home, there was no trace of Ugia. What would he find scattered in bed room were the dismantled parts and wires of robot. It was double whammy for Maan! So she was robot! And whom he had taken for the robot partner of Waru was his partner, Ugia!

The mystery of two skeletons would be unraveled! But Maan had lost his balance in shock swooning down to his bed.

8

Maan was again feeling like homeless. And without any thing to do and everything that could one live for. He was torn by this disability even earlier when Ugia was alive. What happened at Waru home and afterward had just shattered him beyond any possible recovery. Overnight he would be transformed into a numbed and dumb being.

He could not live in the house which was no longer home. The four walls and the overhead roofs and windows seemed to be strangulating him. He would feel his breath choking and gasping for fresh breath of air. Maan would come out in open, setting out in the big, vast and chaotic world.

The dark night greeted him with its eerie silence. The grey night with eerie silence in its belly hazing beyond horizon, broken consistently by traffic noise and hustle and bustle of city life at night. It was almost mid night. And the city life would be in full bloom at night. But where to go? This would bother Maan after wandering for one hour. Above the grey dark sky and below darkness would be in fight with city lights: Night and the world at night seemed to Maan an infinite entity giving solace, rest and peace to humanity for infinite span of time.

Despite uncertainty in the life, it was a good relief from suffocating home of Waru. But his home, for that matter anyone was extension of outside world. The microcosm is as micro as macrocosm is macro. But what is being homeless and how it feels started biting him as chillingly as icy wind blowing over.

Where to go? In such a big and vast world! No place to go? Strange! There must be some place! Even though he would seem to have been displaced from all the places that mattered. Where the body would be leading to, he would be going there! He did not know from where to. But Maan would find himself at a Railway Station. How and why did he reach there he did not know. It seemed as if he were not what he used to be. A new being seemed to have been born inside him. As if legs were taking to him where he found himself and some other self would be watching it like spectator!

The Maan that he once used to be would seem to have melted down into nothing. In that place a new being appeared emerging - new persona that is seeing his body to move, to see, to feel and go wherever wanting to go. As if just he was just an observer seeing his body and its parts, its senses and sense organ doing their respective activities and works. He seemed to have overgrown beyond that Maan who had undergone such trials and travails. Those things did not happen to him, as if someone else was there, not him that would bear such pain and pleasures and ups and downs of life.

He had started feeling lighter. The load and weight of emotions, thoughts, sorrows and happiness all would appear to have gone out to nothingness. He would be a traveler without past baggage. As if the traveler had transformed into being that was not travelling but seeing it happening. And the travelling seemed to have become lighter and smooth.

And that traveler wanted to leave the city for time being. A travel like life journey: destination unknown, travel itinerary not charted. A journey and holiday without any advance booking. There had remained nothing to hold him any longer there.

After ordering tea in nearby stall, Maan took a seat and became a sight of life scene unfolding before him. From nowhere a *Sadhu* appeared and requested Maan to sponsor a cup of tea for him. While he was ordering for him, a *Sanyasi* would come with same request. Then a beggar and vagabond type person.

All were sipping tea and milk with him. There had gathered a motley crowd around him. People were wondering as if they were his extended family. At least it would appear to him. This aroused interest of an American lady. She was looking like young monk. Skin headed, with *Shivaling* tattooed on her forehead, fair and might have been blonde had not shaved her head. First he mistook her for a Sanyasi in white robe. But when she was looking at him admiringly, her beautiful hazel eyes revealing more than what they were trying to conceal. She was the lady beautiful covered in monk dress and outfit.

'Want tea or coffee, Maan asked her.

'Thanks. Could you please help me out? She said rather hesitatingly.

'Yes please …

'Actually..Well… you know, she started hesitatingly but later on got steadied. My Guru needs help, pausing briefly, she continued. Can you please spare some time for him. He is in nearby Ashram.

Maan followed the blonde monk lady in white. She took him to a nearby Ashram. En route to Baba spiritual abode his life story would get unfolded though her, a blind follower of Baba! Her Guru was a *Hathyogi*. He had starved himself for 9 month what he termed as a *Hathyogic Exercise* to control the unbridled senses and the sense organs. After the long self starvation, Baba would be unable to digest anything. Forget the digest; his guts would throw out instantly what was fed.

When they reached Ashram, *Hathyogi* Baba was impatiently awaiting them. That became obvious when he would hand out immediately a long list of medicines, very costly lifesaving drugs and vitamins and tonics. His name was Swami KriyaNand ; I read in his prescription., Kennel- the lady monk was her disciple. He bought some tonics and vitamins and told this what he could afford.

When Kennel told Swami Kriyanand about his inability to foot the bill of all medicines and costly proteins and vitamins, he became rather angry and started arguing about all the charity and bla..bla.... Maan told in no uncertain terms that he was not big person. A jobless, homeless person. Nowhere to go! But he was not ready to listen. And then Baba would start calling names. He began cursing him, with all sort of hermitic bull shit.

After handing the medicines and tonics that he could afford to buy, to Kennel,   he hired a taxi to go to bus station. To leave for Himalayas perhaps. For good! Perhaps!

9

Bus terminus. Maan was awaiting the bus to leave for Himalayas. For good perhaps.! Nothing seemed to be mattering now. Everything and everywhere meaningless and nothingness engulfing the self and beyond .City life and its rampaging crowd, hustle and bustle and pollution were already the constant irritant. Now it had seemed to have reached beyond the toleration level.

Then Kennel appeared coming from nowhere. She might be coming from market side! Sure it was she, but looking very down and low. Then she disappeared from Maan sight. She might be going somewhere else. He was perhaps a little curious to know as to what had happened in Ashram after he left. He was rather peeved, despite helping Baba out, had got his volley of curses in return. It was upsetting him since then.

A strange sense of loneliness would start engulfing Maan's whole being. It would drown him in rather self-cathartic moments of self-probity as to why had happened this and that. What is meaning of life? A vacuum bordering on nothingness would start opening in the answer. The question and answer seemed to be meeting in the vacuums and opening into the blank landscape of nothingness. Void staring at void.

Why it was so that everything had gone wrong. But still life was beckoning him and he was yearning for life. That is why it would be seeking answer in voids and nothingness. And the answer of void will be void. For this reason perhaps why Himalayas would start calling.

Then Kennel again would appear coming from exit gate of Bus Terminus. Perhaps she might be also heading for some place!

'Hi, Kennel came and seated across the bench. She was

looking sad and dejected.

'How is Baba, Maan asked.

She started crying.

'What happened? Maan tried to console her. She got steadied in few moments opening her heart.

'Baba died the moment you left Ashram. He cursed you and it bounced back. He has died and I am feeling like orphan.

She broke into my lap. When she calmed down, we went for coffee and snacks in nearby restaurant.

5
KENNEL ALIAS SWAMI KAMYANAND

Kennel alias Swami Kamyanand was born and brought up in the downtown locality of New York. The all-white locality of hers was sandwiched between black and Asian Locality. Hers was very rough childhood. Sexually violent was her teenage and adulthood. As she had grown up in the multi-racial society she would became rather street smart. In her teenage, she has fallen in love with an Indian guy. It would change the very journey of her life from America to India.

She came to India along with him. They would get married, and everything would be going fine. Until the break up with him. Afterward this rather violent break up, she had come into contact with Swami Hathananad. She was in search of the meaning of life and its purpose. She would visit the spiritual capital of India, Rishikesh.

Kennel was sauntering around. On the serene banks of Ganges, amid the surreal like appearing evening fast descending over the kaleidoscopic mountain tops of the towering Himalayas. The famous evening Aarti of on the banks of serene Ganges with spiraling thousand of diyas, earthen lamps, in synchronism of jingling music of kartal and ghanite. The quite magnificence of serene Ganges water reflecting the dancing earthen lamps would glimpse of creation churning infinitely. There she had met Swami

Hathananad. And she would become his disciple.

Swami Hathananad was a Hathyogi. He wanted to control the volatile senses to attend freedom and Moksha. His basic philosophy was if one wants freedom and happiness in this life, one has to control his or her senses. One day, he decided to put his spiritual philosophy in practice. He would starve himself to control all the senses. For Six month he did not take anything except water.

But after Six month of starvation, his body had developed severe problem. It could not hold any food. The moment he used to eat anything, his ruffled guts would throw it out. Resultantly he fell ill. He was growing weaker and weaker. When Maan met him, he was in the last stage of his life. After getting treatment in a hospital, he was discharged with intensive medication and intake of tonics and vitamins.

Kennel had no sufficient money to buy expensive medicines. She was unable to mange on her own. Maan helped her with whatever money was left after the paying the psychiatrist.

After demise of Baba, Kennel had been rendered homeless. She was feeling like orphan. After his Indian friend ditched her for the arranged marriage, she was left all alone in this alien land. The love for this land of ancient civilizational culture had only remained with her. No money, no job, no home, no friend. She had not sufficient money to go back to her home, America either.

Then she would have found in Baba everything. A Guru, father, mother and lover secretly, everything! It was sort of relation like that of god and soul. This was Kennel side of story. Baba's was just in wreck. It was for perhaps this reason that Baba had announced his suicidal vow of no food for six month.

Kennel was not aware that Baba was just infatuated with her. The day she came to the Ashram, he had fallen in love with her. But he would try to conceal that Kennel did not miss to find. But for his obstinate mind that did not accept it. He himself had pooh pooled it as mere Vishay Vaasana or the play of senses.

But the inmates of Ashram could not fail to notice the growing passion and restlessness of Baba. Her coming to Ashram had posed a challenge to Baba. His whole Babadom was in doldrums. His uncontrollable infatuation for her had challenged his very Babadom. And He was in virtual revolt of himself. His senses, mind and heart had been rendered at discord with each other.

The problem with senses is that if one rises in revolt, other follows the suit. It becomes like virtual opening of the floodgates, unbalancing the very life. Baba had left the world but the world had not left him. The ego and mind conditioning he could not surmount. His whole being and that of his disciples were founded on renouncement of world that had not left them, and would keep them throwing unbalanced most of the time. Even though they had left it at face value!

When Kennel came, Baba controlled sexuality would explode like silent inactive volcano. Her charm and sensuousness had overwhelmed him. He would just get stuck up in it. For many days he would try to control his unbound sexuality. In many sleepless nights he would venture out in her room. But at the last moment, sanity would save him from what could have been another scandal.

The very sight of Kennel would excite Baba. Her soft and scintillating voice used to make him mad. He had become so fascinated with her that very thought of her would put his whole being on fire of passion. It had something to do with his troubled and repressed adult hood.

He belonged to very conservative traditional family. The woman folks would always be in Purdah. If anyone seen without it, even at home it was considered outrageous to the morality and general sensibility of the family. Once he was caught masturbating by his father, and for that he was given severe punishment and chastisement by father for a long period.

He was kept on the semi-starvation stage for one year. No interaction with opposite sex. Even not with that of own family member! The penance was such that even the most ascetic type would flinch.

Thus the foundation for future Sanyasi or Baba would be laid down. And it had started taking shape ever since then. The more he would try to repress his sexuality more explosive it would be becoming day by day. When he had attained full adulthood, he would all of sudden decide to become Sanyasi. And soon he would renounce the world by announcing his intent to the stunned family members.

But Kennel had disturbed his life. His whole existence would be torn between two. And his whole being would like ebbing and exploding tides stuck up in these opposites of have and not have Kennel. The more he tried to control, more it would become a sort of vicious circle. And he decided for the fast of 9 months.

PART
3

1
CAVES TO KINGDOM OF LIFE

1

Maan in no man's land of existence! He was neither being himself and nor becoming to be . No being and doing. Even if for time being! The moment of not being in any of the being would linger on as if for the eternity. The eternity of nothingness and being, and incubating the potentiality of new being!

He had landed in the land of Kinnaur- Lahaul Spiti. He was fleeing from himself as well from the world. The law of motion and change notwithstanding, could anyone flee from himself or herself? It's like fleeing from one's own shadow. More one fleets from it more it shadows over us. More so when world is but extension of self: outside is but the extension of inside and the inside that of outside. The difference is in mind not spatial.

The highest village of world-Tibia! Up above the mountains of higher Himalayas and in the lap of sky! A toy of nature it would appear like, playing with infinity in the lap of nature. Day and night amidst snow capped mountains it has been swinging since time memorial! Maan would feel like out to stir and play with it. He but could not help lost in the toy land of nature.

He would see from afar beautiful lass tending her Yaks, goats and sheep. A desire to see her from near would stir him to new life. Maan would be right on the path leading to go, off from a precipice of unfathomable gorge to vantage point. All of sudden he would feel like settling here for good.

Mesmerized by beauty and splendor of higher Himalayas, Maan would feel like as if he had got what he was seeking. But again the memories and association of thoughts would pull him back to his scary past. The past he left behind would start haunting.

The problem of human nature seems to be the seeing everything from memory and thoughts, missing the beauty and happiness unfolding at the present moment. Every moment and every instance has its own aura and existence. These cannot be measured and seen from memory and experience as these are rooted in the past. And in the time and space gone by! Every thought and experience is in the time and it goes stale with time.

But for Maan, these were new things happening to him amid the indescribable beauty of Himalayas. He felt like as if he could live here. Life could be lived here as it was with Kajal and other lovers and beloveds. Life prospect with its attendant immense possibilities would start looking bright to him. Even if for time being!

Maan had come here after parting company from Kennel at Rewalsar. They had gone to Rewalsar together from Delhi and decided to settle there.

Rewalsar- A beautiful Buddhist place located aside the lake. It was the abode of all branches of Buddhism, but predominantly Tibetan Buddhists. The monks and the tourists from foreign country would visit here frequently. In winter the Lama people living in higher Himalayas would flock here to escape the harsh winter there.

Kennel had become Buddhist. She was enamored of its pacifist and middle path teachings. She had joined the leading Tibetan monastery at Rewalsar. She had even started living therein like monks. She would silently be chanting on the beads and taking numerous rounds around the sacred lake of Rewalsar. It was difficult to differentiate her with other Buddhists. With shaven head and in Lama Robe, she would become center of attention.

And Maan would stay in the nearby hotel. He was trying to be what he did not want to be. The memory and thoughts of past life, the pain and agony that he got in search of happiness! And lure of banal and carnal freedom and multiplicity would be haunting him, like it would never ever leave him. More he tried to repress it, more it would become acute. 'I think therefore exist' would be becoming albatross claw in his neck.

He would have existed in better way had not he thought to suppress these agonizing memory and thoughts that would be bothering him.

More he thought more his existence would get ensnared in non-existence. His thinking to not think about these would be further adding up to the cacophonous crowd of thoughts and memories, choking his self further down the painful memory lane of his life.

'Maan! You also become monk like me, said Kennel one morning when she was taking the round along with him around the sacred lake.

The bright morning with its golden rays had colored the lake, narrow valley and cool sentinels of peace like mountains in its golden hues. The blue sky above was adding to the golden hue that nature had taken, filling with hope and aspiration for life.

'This you call life...chanting and chanting ...monotony of constantly suppressing life and worldly things, said Maan with inexplicable irritation. This is the life! And it is meaning? You living the life or leaving it? Just unable to understand.

'Oh dear! Just give a try. Chant, pray, meditate. Life would come back to you, Kennel pleaded.

'Okay. Will give a try..., Maan replied with diffidence and skepticism.

But it would prove to be a futile proposition from the very beginning. The chanting and meditation was unable to heal the bruised psyche of Maan. Why should he control thoughts and how, chanting and mediation would make any impact, he would be unable to understand. It had added to the chaos within him, Maan would think more often than not.

How could life be a nothing and heap of sorrow, and how could it be waded through! If everything is illusion, then viewing it as such is also illusion: he would often be wondering. For that matter why life would have been created if there would be misery, sorrow and nothingness. Something wrong in our perception or thinking or misunderstanding!

They say you would get liberation and joy at the end of life! But if one gets happiness and liberation from cycle of sorrow and happiness at the end of life, then what it would be of use if life is near its end. Till this stage is reached, keep on suffering and struggling to ward of this futility of life!

A disciple of Buddha had asked *Tathagat*: what he would get after liberation. He said nothing, instead he had left everything. When another disciple asked where would be he after death, he said: nowhere. It means he will be everywhere, united with Braham or Super Being or nothingness. So for a seeker it may or may not come at end as everyone can not be as lucky as Buddha. Even if he or she attains the liberation, life would be near its fag end of journey.

What we would get at the end would be nothing! Meanwhile the life would be lived expending on emptying everything, ridding of what life provides. For that one elusive end, every moment of life would be sacrificed for the succeeding moments. And at the end, what one would get nothing and nothingness because, as they say life has come out from nothingness and goes out to the nothingness.

Then why does one not live from beginning as nothing: egoless, taking ups and down, happiness and sorrow in their fullness with equanimity, leaving everything to life and existence without undue fascination for one or other, leaving its fruits and result on Him, as Krishna or soul theory believes, did. This cathartic thinking going within Maan would provide him some hope.

But Maan was unable to find any tangible solace. Nothing would seem to be appealing to him: Everything in life and of world would appear insignificant, at least for time being. And meaninglessness would often creep from nowhere, shading the life with grey color. He was confused with changing colors of thoughts and evanescent immanence.

Everything is fleeting, Maan would think sitting on a rock near the meadow of dry grassland and rocks. Time is fleeting. Earth is moving away from stars; stars from universe. Body fleeting from childhood to youth, to old age to death and then again new cycle beginning! Every being is fleeting from previous beings. Everything is moving from one point to another. And self is fleeting from me, and life seems to be living or lost in between!

Maan would feel as if he were never been: always fleeting from one point to another. From one being to another, one desire to another, chasing one dream to another, from one girl to another, and on and on. Why this feeling of fleeting? Is it because he is pointless: nothing to do, nowhere to go? A pointless being among multitudes of points! That is the predicament of life or life itself: a pointless being, nothingness, zero, vacuum, a void. Just be what is! Just be, present living in every moment, leaving everything to Him. Or karma or cause and effect

That seemed to be essence of life for Maan: the sum total of all his life. Everything attained: all freedom, multiplicity, all shades of colors. Pleasure and more pleasure followed by pain and more pain. There was gain and more gaining followed by the loss and kept on losing. Riches, poverty, beauty and filth! Everything gone and what remained: only debris, void and nothingness.

Whether life is void and we try to fill this void with new being that again results into void! So why not be like void or void itself, Maan was thinking while returning from the highest village of world to the void less void!

2

Kaza: A city in the cold desert. At the altitude of 20000 ft., surrounded by snowcapped baron mountain ranges touching the blue sky line like sentinel of beauty, and without vegetation, any tree and capped with snow laden peaks reflecting sunlight soaking the valleys in golden hue . A dazzling and simmering beauty would be appealing to eyes at the same time.   Some apple trees and shrubs scattered over the brown and reddish landscape providing greenish succor to barren landscape.

Maan was sauntering around the cold desert town. It appeared like toy of nature amidst barren wilderness. An oasis in desert, dust storm rising at the drop of hat—even light wind giving rise to massive dust storm. A vehicle passed by choking him with dust. He thought it better to go towards market.

Kaza market spread over the zigzagging steeped gully was bustling with people and all sorts of wares of domestic and agricultural uses. In the wilderness it appeared like fair. Maan was just doing window shopping in the heart of market. He saw two women haggling over the price of some ware with shopkeeper. He but could not help to look at the two women in nomad dress and laden with all sort of beads and stones. The one with blue eyed and in grey tribal dress caught his attention. She was haggling with shopkeeper over the price of product she had purchase. A teenage girl in red dress was standing behind her.

When Maan came near to them, he found that that the girl was sort of some money. And shopkeeper was not willing to give vegetable knife despite her pleading with folded hands. A motley crowd of passersby had started gathering there, more to see the dazzling beauty of two nomad women than to sort out the running quarrel. Then Maan stepped into:

'How much money? He asked to shopkeeper.

'Ten, pat came the reply of shopkeeper. Taking out a note of Rs 10, he gave it to him. The women went away happily, thanking him with long side glances.

Maan could not stay for long in Kaza. The dust and dry cold

was choking life out of him. There he got friendly with a Sadhu or wandering Sanyasi who was from Manali. He suggested going to Tabo; there he would find peace and solace.

'Babuji take it, offering a cannabis joint Babaji said, You will feel better.

As Maan was choking with dust and high altitude sickness, he but could not resist the offer. After taking two three puff, Maan felt as if he were transported to the seventh heaven. All worries, all problems of life and anxiety about future seemed to have gone away as if they were never there. A new enthusiasm for life would start descending.

'Babaji! Its nice to see Hindu Sanyasi in the land of Lama, said Maan taking one more puff from cannabis joint...

'When I have renounced the world, replied Baba. How does it matter whether one is Hindu *Sanyasi* or Buddhist? All ways are same.

'But why did you renounce the world, Maan interrupted him.

'World is not worth living. There is nothing but sorrow and sorrow. Everything is illusion ....

Babaji started narrating his life story. But Maan was wondering if world is not worth living, why and how world has been created. If life is not worth living, why he is living? Perhaps he is living by renouncing the world. Maan was unable to understand.

But Maan was sure he had not renounced the world. He had come here to live life, see what life is in store for him.

He departed for Tabo.

3

When Maan reached Tabo from Kaza, evening was descending with all its splendor and beauty. He stopped at tri-junction of town, feeling as if he had arrived at tri-pod of his life. Three routes seemed to be opening before his eyes.

The first route was beckoning him back to past modern life, going back to the juncture he had left behind. Back to urban chaos. Hoards of choices and desires to reek in. Freedom of unrestricted life and no hold barred life styles, multiplicity of beings and lives, not one truth but many truths. Pleasure of body, matter only mattering, conscience and soul is dead. So is god and godliness, consumerism becoming new god: eat drink and be merry. And effect Maan knew better than anyone: burnt bridges of life and being.

Then Maan saw appearing from far beyond high snowcapped mountains of Lahaul Spiti, a life route. A big blank slate or blackboard like route of life: to live afresh, to write and rewrite again, without bothering about the cemented matrix, about space and result: it can be wiped clean for writing again. With no tension for space to be written again, life is to be lived again with any expectation of getting overwritten (result).

And third was not visible. Then a dry leave having fallen on earth came blowing with wind from road going towards world's oldest monastery of Tabo. A dry leave flying and grounding in wind of Prarabdh (the cumulative sum of one's karma and its effect). Having fallen from his branch (Super Soul or Super being) dry leave (soul encased in a body) letting it to be to the life forces. No tension, giving hoot to what would happen to it.

Wherever and whenever wind takes, flying or grounding,

to water or back water, to up above mountains and horizon in tempest he goes. Without any effect resultant of its blowing at beck and command of wind and other elements. But he remains the dry leave of tree whether frozen in snowfall or cold desert.

'Bhaiya! Want a room or guest house"

Maan looked back in the direction the sweet voice coming from. A beautiful Spiti girl was standing in portico of Guest house, LahaulSpiti with Tabo restaurant written on signboard. It was off the read winding through Tabo town, to up above towards Tabo monastery.

It appeared nice guest house. With panoramic view of Lahaul Spiti Mountains surrounding it and lapping the guest house with magnificence of sublime and beautiful. And Maan decided to check in.

The room had panoramic view of Lahaul Spiti Mountains, facing valley with Small Township and the golden dome of ancient monastery shining and reflecting the spiritual aura. *Budham shranam gachhami* seemed to be ringing atop from the oldest monastery. Overwhelmed with this, Maan just lied down on bed observing the spiritual and natural beauty unfolding before his eyes. The ancient history of Buddhism and its rise and fall in India despite its success abroad started coming filtered through most ancient monastery of Tabo.

Solitude of solemnity and coolness started cooling frayed temper of Maan. The solitude of gratitude towards nature and her forces and it was certainly not that of desolation and loneliness that used to haunt him no longer there. The dry leave was cooling its heels, taking cool and peaceful swinging of life: the spiritual aura filtering through glass window of guest house swinging and lulling him into trance like sleep.

There was knocking at door.

'Yes, Maan coming out of trance.

There slowly entered the owner lady of the guest house, followed by his daughter with tray of hot tea and a glass of water. The one was in her 40s and other in 20s. Spitian beauty with reddish hair color and slim figure!

'We offered this room to you on nominal rate, said the lady sitting on upholstered sofa. As you are painter and we are from good family.

The daughter also nodded in affirmation with sly and tender smile. She was standing beside her mother. Maan asked her to sit down. She was beautiful and tender like red rose bud. Then her 16 year old son also came, sitting silently beside her. The guest house and adjacent restaurant was being run by family. The father was at reception.

'We have made it for foreigners, said the owner lady about the room. It's very costly but giving you being artist.

The guest house was built in Swiss cottage style. The room was atop of it presenting penthouse like view. The artist in Maan was born when he was checking in guest house. When Mr. Tong, husband of the landlady asked about his profession while filling entries at reception:

'Artist, Maan said randomly.

But he did not know then that he would have to redeem the lie by impregnating his being with seed of artist. The first thing that he did when he went out for walk was to buy sketch book and sketch pens and pencils. And for two three days he was busy in making sketches and drawings. New life energy was bestowing him with passion and zeal for life.

4

It was the third day in Lahaul Spiti guest house. Maan seated on sofa was busy making sketches. In his sketch book lying on center table, facing the snowcapped mountains, a Spiti lass was descending on the canvas. He was not sure whether it was mother- Mrs. Tong or daughter- Miss Tong.

Whoever might be, their fascinating sublime beauty was emerging through lines and figures onto sketch book. Like fairies coming down to the earth from fairyland: The ancient monastery with its golden hue in the backdrop of bluish mountains standing in infinite shadow of crystal blue sky in background. A landscape portrait in making or what he could not anticipate.

Once a work of art begins, the artist (or writer) and art becomes a process just like life is process of cause and effect moving on their own. The artist becomes the medium of the creative forces and their dynamics. The artist gives in to art and its dynamism. When artist tries to interfere with this self propelled process with his or her subjectivity, it gets derailed and what will come out not creativity but mundane and routine. Maan was a sort of ad hoc artist. He was not aware of these things.

There entered Miss Tong, 18 years old daughter of Mrs. Tong, the lady owner of guest house, looking less than 14 years old; tip toeing on her long legs with lightly curvaceous slanderous Greek body. Her pinkish fair cheeks were flushed with tenderness of red rose bud.

'What are you painting, said Miss Tong in her soft husky voice, sounding like melodious Bulbul humming for her partner?

'Nothing, Maan tried to hide the sketch with awkwardness of a lover whose love was about to be revealed to his beloved.

But Miss Tong had seen it arousing her virginal curiosity and passion. Brimming with innocence of virgin beauty she tried to snatch it plunging headlong on him. Before the dry leave crackles under soft and alluring weight of a virgin beauty, Maan wrested himself from her passionate plunge and sat down on bed. Lo and behold, she was again unto him to take a peep into sketch.

The moment of flesh meeting flesh would linger on as if for eternity. The moment was fast multiplying into instants and instant into years and years into millennium of carnal desire. The innocence was on offer as if to get deflowered into carnal and banal passion of flesh. But Maan was holding on to the edge of precipice of carnal desire. He was being wary of repeating the past escapades with girls and women. And even bi experience. Even if the precipice was alluring despite all the dangers, the edge was not nudging to go for insatiable lust.

The sketch was her mother's: a nude beauty. And the inspiration for that had come from her chance encounter of her bathing yesterday. The bathroom door was partly opened. And her body splashing with water; and Maan had gone their side of residence to ask for a bottle of mineral water. As none was at reception, he thought to go their residence which was behind the reception.

And there she was having bath and her bathing beauty was coming filtered through partly opened door. She thought her husband had come from restaurant. The shower was not working properly and she wanted her husband to look into it. When door opened, Maan got stuck up in that scene and moment unfolding the naked beauty with fairness of her body glistening, well shaped breast, the curls and curves. Having noticed Maan, she would become a marble statue, being chiseled for the sake of a beauty to be partaken.

The time and place had melted in that moment. Many moments flashed in that moment: a thousand scenes were moving with fast cuts. That moment also lingered like this moment when Miss Tong was trying to snatch the sketch from Maan. And he not giving away, she would pile over Maan who was stretching on his back to avoid her. But she would be adamant at having a look on that picture. She was not relenting her efforts to snatch sketch form his stretched out hand. And Maan was not allowing her to do so. Meanwhile that fleshy moment would keep lingering on.

Then came her mother voice searching for her daughter: Tingi…Tingi

She hurriedly released Maan from her soft burden. But the mother did not fail to notice their escapade.

'What's happening, she looked at Baby Tong suspiciously. She left the room in huff.

'Actually she was adamant to see the half finished sketch, Maan said showing the sketch.

She would start decoding the sketch. Then she exclaimed with joy of model looking herself in the portrait by artist: oh it's me! She hugged so passionately and tightly that Maan felt as if she would never ever release him. The passion was running amok: from hug to kissing, and the lightning of rustling dresses, thunder of two desperate to be one; clouds were to rain….

Thence would come the voice of her teenage son, looking for his mother. The mother hurriedly exited leaving future lover gasping for passion. The dormant passion first aroused by the virginal beauty and left in lurch for the adult. The adult taking it to penultimate of foreplay, arousing tempest of passion to hilt left for fending for itself. And the fiend of passion was now baying for his beloved's teenaged son.

Maan would feel like sodomizing him for the perceived debauchery of his mother and sister. Not only him, but his father and ..... .

It was becoming too much for him. His whole life seemed to be at stake. The repeat of past with more malicious debauchery was struggling to find space in his being. Lolita and Lolita in reverse and Lolita in obverse and Lolita for no hold barred......

Maan barged outside to reconnect the inside with outside. The connecting line had snapped endangering the very existence his being.

5

Maan was out in Tabo. The Inside had colored the outside as well. The question was how to de-color the inside and detangle it form snaring of the outside. The outside might help in sanitizing the inside. But inside and outside intersecting each other: the inside in outside and the outside in inside! What to do?

He was out in the wilderness again. The dry leave was flying in the typhoon of inside: out in the outside colored with inside.

Maan was feeling like the king of Naggar castle thrown outside with the fast wind of change! He would have certainly tried to prevent outside enveloping the inside. But how could inside remain immune from outside! Maan was wondering how the king would have felt when he came to know that he would have to leave the castle forever. He was more concerned with leaving than living-building new castle. The new castle could be built if not too much attached with old one.

But the king was fascinated and attached with beauty and comfort of castle. He could not think about anything else. He left the castle and did not build another. While his castle was rotting, the king gone and new king yet to come, he was building castle in air.

Man was wondering whether he is king or castle. Or king in castle or castle in king: outside in inside or inside in outside. He could not ascertain the predicament he was in or predicament was he himself. He was disgusted with himself- a sort of self-loathing. A fear that it might be beginning of sleazy past that he had emptied out long from the self and his life. That left out past was threatening to haunt him more severely.

How can one flee from form self? One can flee person and place, but it is just impossible to flee from oneself. The self remains constant and more one wants to flee from it, more it haunts, giving rise to a conflict and putting very existence of being in danger zone.

Maan was passing through a tempest. An inner conflict that cool and serene outside of Spiti could not silence. The serene and spiritual aura would be unable to cool his burning passion for the daughter, mother, son and father as well. He knew it was wrong and morally, ethically outrageous. More he thought about it, more it would give rise to inner conflict.

He was walking randomly. He had reached the northern most part of Tabo. The river Sutlej flowing quietly: Very different from its ferocious and violent flow down the stream. The same river but its different nature, Maan was thinking, gazing across the brown and grey mountain with ancient caves dotting the foothills.

Same life is there but the different beings. Is life in another's hands decided, shaped by nature, environment and society. So human being is nothing but product of his nature and nurture, environment. Destiny or design or freedom! Then where is self, Maan was wondering.

'I think therefore I exist' seems to have meshed up the life with the crowding of thoughts and being lost to these unfounded and vexatious thoughts, ideas and beings. Existence, for Maan seemed to have exited in the multiplicity of thoughts, desires and beings. Maan was not aware about that being has been left to fend for itself in vast and chaotic universe of immanence-what is called *bhavsagar* in Hindu tradition. That too being is without any oars of transcendence-self control, any negotiating entity inside (Soul) that could mediate upon. But Maan was developing this faculty unknowingly even if it was in the initial stage.

Moderns like Maan are not to be faulted. The modernity seems to be culprit. The replacement of God, Soul and transcendence or knowledge (Gyan in Hindi) with new gods of ideology, rituals and social dos and dents, technology, Kingdom of God, Swarg, Jannat and all superstitions, closed ideology, dogmatism and materialism and consumerism perhaps is hollowing the being and their existence.

Maan oblivious of these was sitting on grey black rock on the bank of Sutlej River, dividing Spiti valley in two- Tabo and Kaza. Lost as he was in the reveries of unknown forces of life, suddenly the ancient caves at the foot and middle of grey mountains of Spiti started vibrating with some sort of attraction for him.

The crystal blue sky overhead would be making an infinite arch resting on the finite mountains of Lahaul Spiti. They appeared beckoning him. Strange, Maan was thinking, If destiny or design, without choice and transcendence (gyan he knowingly meant), then where is self? Why caves seem to be calling?

He was not aware that life is what it is: as it unfolds before us as it is, bound by infinite play of cause and effect, karma. One has to move in life making good of the good and bad things as well. With transcendence or Gyan, leaving everything to karma or to operations of the cause and effect or God seems only viable way-out from this existential dram that life is. Design or destiny is there but one has to make choice to shape that design or destiny.

Mann had also one choice to make right there, sitting alone in the wilderness of awesome beauty: where to go. Even that was not available at that time, and he had to make choice. Destiny or design or karma had thrown him into open and choice was his to make. Even if that did not seem to be available at that time, he had to exert to make so. He could not go back to castle of Mrs Tong.

There were many self made demons of forbidden desire lurking in the castle: LGBTQIA redux, and relapsing to vicious circle of modernity that has made the empowerment of gender and sexuality of freedom as life style-misnomer for freedom perhaps.

Other options of going back to hustle and bustle of metropolitan life had been ticked before. And then what to do? Maan had to decide as the shadows of evening had started casting its dark net. Afternoon seemed to be eager to give way to the evening. The shadows hovering around the inside was giving it even darker shade.

Maan having found no place to go and anything to do, started walking randomly. And awkwardly too! Then he found himself moving towards ancient caves dotting the foothills of the mountain. The graying mountain evening was fast descending, the chill and fear of darkness was enveloping the valley and mountains. The sparkling beauty of Sutlej was graying too. He started moving fast as if there was running competition between the fast approaching evening and his legs.

There appeared a makeshift of tent cave, lighted amidst grey darkness. His joy would know no bound. Smoke was wafting through chimney of makeshift tent cave. So life is there amidst no man's land of wilderness, Maan but could not fail to feel happy. With a sigh of relief!

6

The make shift tent-cave belonged to Kaal. And Kaal seemed to be deserter of modern life. Like Maan in conventional sense. But Kaal did not think so. He had come to the wilderness, as he told to Maan, to find the meaning in life. Life is meaning itself and if one tries to seek meaning in the meaning, whether it would be found or not, is debatable. Kaal was out in wilderness to get his life on board, derailed by its exigencies. He was perhaps postponing the meaning of life that Maan could not know.

When Kaal was born, as he confided to Maan, there was a frown on his face. The infantile frown that turned unnatural frowns as he grew his years. And it shadowed his personality adding frown after frown in his life. His father was teacher and mother housepartner belonging to a rich family. As father was unable get her partner conceived, they adopted a newly born son of a distant relative having half a dozen kids. Thus Kaal was born from adopted mother. They kept it well guarded secret for fear of society scorn and frown.

When Kaal was born, their parents, Kamini and Kaaldev were in Madhupur. A bordering town on the Hills of Chhotanagpur plateau-the world oldest mountains, now reduced to the plateau.. It was not coincidence that town used to be holiday resort of Rabindrnath Tagore, the world famous Nobel laureate poet. His brother had built a castle which was of some tourists interest as the Nobel laureate used to come during summer. He had also written some stanza of award winning collection of poems, Gitanjali.

Every place, geographical location, town, metropolitan, village has unique magnetic field having some or other effects on individual. Astrology also believes every star and planet has some influence on human beings. It may be taken with a pinch of salt, but Kaal wanted to be poet. He was fascinated with hills and jungle. He could not understand why he wanted to be poet, and hills and jungles used to make him mad with joy and inexplicable happiness.

Kaal's life right from beginning has been rather bizarre: an endless saga of shadows, shadowy things! A sort of shadow chasing that his life appeared from hindsight. From one shadow to another, he had been going after, taking them as real. But at the end, he would find them to be shadow. A sort of mirage in desert: from a distant it was real, when he went near, it would keep shifting to further and further. And now shadow chasing had brought him in the wilderness. In wilderness he was seeking life and its meaning, while in the real life he had been seeking mirage, shadow and wilderness.

'how come you are living in wilderness, Maan asked looking beyond the abandoned caves, adding to the wilderness. Shadows seemed to have disappeared or united with shadow.

' Living in wilderness is also about life, said Kaal pouring tea in two cups and passing to Maan. Cheers to life in wilderness!

'I did not get what you are saying, Maan said sipping tea from his cup.

'There is wilderness within the wilderness, replied Maan putting his cup on side table. One is within and without as well. One can feel the violence of wilderness even in crowd and feel crowded in the peace of wilderness. The wilderness without is reality while within it is tangible truth. Is not a jungle within that is spread over without….

Maan was blank. He could not make any sense out of it.

'You are Buddhist, Maan was exerting himself to understand what Kaal was saying about.

'Not exactly… but Buddhism and Hinduism are two side of one coin. One considers nothing as God while other everything as God. One reality becoming all before coming out form nothing, coming from nothingness and going to nothingness or becoming one with that. One believes in Nirgun Brahma, other in Sagun…

'What is Brahma, Maan asked with ignorance of innocent.

'Its God having everything within …its all everything right form a stone to humans… its like solitude.., Kaal trying to simplify the reality hoping Maan to understand it.

'Solitude..Really..How come… Maan exclaimed.

'In solitude you are not alone but merged with whole world. And that is what Brahma is…… Kaal stopped sermon in wilderness seeing Maan gaping blankly.

'Ok ...forget everything, said Kaal after a pause. Just be silent and listen to what solitude is conveying to ...

Both fell silent. The silence of Tabo outskirts would start engulfing the tent cave. Kaal and Maan were sitting silently in their tent cave. Through its cut out window the valley bathed in moon had sneaked there in, becoming the part of all round silence. The mystic silence of the ancient caves was adding to the prevailing silence.

The snowcapped grey mountains of Lahaul Spiti standing still, majestically soaked in the cool moonshine. The valley bathed in lukewarm dreamy coolness of moon appeared to be stretching to the outside from inside. The outside would have merged into the inside! Even river appeared to be flowing in hushed silence with thousand moons floating in its moony water.

Maan silently would be overtaken by a sort of stupor, the inside becoming outside and the outside inside, all differences seemed to have apparently gone. The seer seemed to have become seen and the scene. A glimpse of one reality enveloping all: a unified field of existence. The eyes seeing these mountains and valley, the self would be just nowhere or everywhere as it was observing these realities. Even the self appearing as mountains, valley, river and sky with moon, it's his projection or they exist because the self making them to be, by seeing it through eyes!

A glimpse of beyond! Time and space blurred, all coming from one reality and going out in it, looking like one at sublime level. Inside seemed to be stretching to the outside and the outside being permeated by the inside. As if it's happening in the realm going beyond the time and space! The song of solitude singing, making it difficult for Maan to discern the singer and sung and song: like an ode to solitude.

Solitude, solitude! Away from multitude, no attitude, no ego, no thinking: only solitude. Magnitude becoming multitude! No attitude, no latitude. All melting in solitude and solitude in all, one becoming all and all looking like one. Bang or Big bang coming out of solitude and melting into it with all stars, planets and galaxy, lives animate or inanimate living in solitude prevailing thereafter. Even before life solitude reigning and after it going into solitude. And then nothing but solitude only!

Maan was no longer feeling lonely and alone in the world. On contrary a feeling of fulfillment and gratitude towards life and existence would engulf him, making it feel like cool and happy. And Kaal was time personified pervading all the present, past and future of life. Life itself: both gross and subtle.

7

Maan stay at Kala world of the make shift tent-cave lingered on. Till eternity it seemed to Maan. The instant would be stretching to the day and the day to night, to week, month, years and centuries, and on and on. Even though it was his only second day out there!

Maan would feel as if he had been knowing Kaal since the ages! Even if he had been acquainted with him yesterday only! But Kaal would appear to have been always his acquaintance, friend of his: like two birds living in one nest or the cave of life. Similar and at the same time dissimilar to Plato's cave, where what is inside cave is shadow of outside but unlike his cave the inside shadow is that of inside apparently looking like that of outside. It is only due to illusion it is appearing different. Maya and Brahma but Maya (illusion that is life) is itself within and outside less Brahma- apparently looking different but one reality.

Kaal would not tell Maan that he was a sort of living volcano. His being had been always as if out to burst burning his finger as that of the body-world. He had a plan, a vision to factor the world and its cultures and civilization. When he revealed it , showed to world, world had termed him mad.

The situation he would find himself in was something like a sane person going to a place inhabited by blinds. When he told them they had lost their vision, he was hounded and howled by them. And finally the man was termed as super blind. Such would be vision that could further botch up their blindness by making them deaf.

Kaal knew time was not right for the volcano to burst. He was bidding his time. Few days back there were tremors after tremors. It appeared he could no longer check this volcano to burst forth out in the world. Hence he had to come here or brought forth, he was not sure.

Maan often used to wonder as to what had made Kaal to come here. He but could not fail to marvel at the ingenuity of Kaal. Reclining on easy chair beside the cutout window of tent- cave, Maan used to look into outside beauty engulfing the wild and lonely stretch of Lahaul Spiti. Sometime like enchanted onlooker and other time as observer. While Kaal would be always busy in some or other activity. Some time he would be writing, other time mediating, reading and on and on. And Maan would just see him doing all and feeling like as he if was doing!

One eerie afternoon! Maan was lost in the unfolding scene of the outside. He forgot that he was Maan. He would be everything-mountains, valley, rocks, trees and shrubs, and even Yak, goats and sheep. He seemed to have transformed into all pervading, all permeating observer soul like. Unknowingly, had he known it would not have happened!

Maan forgetting Maan!And becoming one with all! The seer and seen divide appeared melting , becoming all pervading and permeating observer like being. He felt as if he would be situated in soul, what is called in Hindi '*Atmsthit*'. He was not body but soul in body and that of all beings! Even that of non-sentient beings!

'Want anything? Going for long mediation, Kaal was calling from his bedside. But Maan felt as if his voice were travelling from afar and he had not heard it.

Yes, he is Kaal, man born with frown on forehead. The news about his birth mark, frown spreading like wild fire. People of all sorts started visiting his house to see the frown. And countless stories and speculation started doing round. Some said it was omen of good luck, other said it would bring misfortune and calamities. There were faithful and zealots terming as sign of devil, while other saw it as mark of demi god.

Kaal's adopted mother, Kamini became very anxious. The destiny was playing trick on her! She could not help herself from thinking. First she was tied to stone who could not keep her happy and give her offspring. When she adopted a son secretly and making people believe that he was born to them, this frown and its bad omen had started worrying her. Her husband tried to console but in vain.

Maan's mother worry was growing day by day. One day Maan father's friend, teacher by profession, told her about a mystic and philosopher, Mullah Nasiruddin who was born laughing. Krishn was also said to be born with a smile. He said there must be some hidden meaning of this frown on Kaal's forehead. Maan's mother, Kamini got more scared than soothed down.

A fortune teller, Panduranga was called forth. What he foretold about Kaal would sooth her mother anxiety and worry a bit. But it would give rise to unending rituals, superstition and dogmatism. 'What he foretold about Maan proved to be a turning point in the life of all and sundry.

This boy is avtar of Mother Goddess Kali and would destroyer of demons and evil forces. Once Ma Kaali got so enraged, Panduranga was telling, that it appeared that she would destroy whole world. While slaying demon and evil forces, she in her anger forgot to differentiate between good and evil. Then her consort, Lord Shiva lied down in her path. And when she found him lying down in her path, she realized her mistake and thus was world saved from imminent annihilation.

Kaal had some feminine quality of womanhood as well. He would chart a new course in human history. He would bring change in the society and world, Panduranga was reading his fortune. Like Goddess Kaali he would destroy the bad and evil forces, bringing reform in his own religion and make it universal religion.

Now her mother got worried about his safety. Anyone could harm him and nip her tender bud. She requested Panduranga not to reveal these thing to anybody. But he was being non-committal in this regard, for the reason best known to him. There was something cooking up in his mind perhaps!

'Please Panduranga! Don't reveal these things to anybody, Kaal adopted mother was pleading with him with folded hand. But he was ducking it, sitting tight-lipped. Perhaps he had seen good opportunity to make fortune in cash and kind.

'Why are you worried, said Panduranga casting his net over unsuspecting gullible mother. This is matter of glory... your son is ....,

'Please! I beg you, said her mother falling over his feet. Don't reveal... She placed her head over ankles, revealing her cleavages from maxi. Her bust was softly touching his knees and Panduranga was in seventh heaven without any penance or sacrifice. He started patting her hair. Still he was non-committal to her pleadings.

Panduranga was not saying anything, she was thinking. There must be some reason. Her mind was getting disturbed with foreboding. He would reveal it to others putting her adopted son life in danger. She did not let out the soft touch of her body tucked between his two legs. It was not that she did not realize the intention of Panduranga in not replying to her. He was gently patting her head and enjoying the softness of her body. And her adopted son Maan was peeping through his room into drawing room.

Kaal's father was away for a month. He had been transferred to remote area. And Kamini decided to stay put here for future of her adopted son. She did not allow to ruin his career by shifting to the place without proper education facilities and career building. She would stay put here with her adopted son. Kaal was almost crossing his twelfth year and was in seventh grade. He had grown up a handsome and tall boy. He was strong and taller than her weakling and small statured husband. She just loved him for that.

Kaal was peeping through door: her adopted mother was enjoying the carnal blessings of Panduranga, resting her body on his knees. He was giving blessings to her with his eyes shut and patting her head and down to her back. She started pushing her body against his legs and waist, seated as he was on sofa and she on carpet. She was expecting that Panduranga would take initiative. But he was afraid of losing the ground he had got over her. And this foreplay disguised in blessing and blessed lingered on.

8

Kamini, Kraal's adoptee mother was a god fearing lady, having some sense of morality. She was devout worshipper of goddess Kali, and Panduranga was aware of this. For this reason perhaps he was not being pro-active in seducing her. She had almost surrendered to him: but he was unable to move fearing her strict sense of morality.

Panduranga was reclining on sofa, eyes closed, Kamini sitting on carpet below the sofa. Her face buried in his lap, seeking his commitment that not coming forth.

'Your son destiny would benefit more, Panduranga said patting her back with one hand. If more people will come to know. It would make.... He lost his words as he had taken Kamini on his both legs and started swinging her like child.

Kamini opened her eyes and tried to look askance at him. But his eyes were closed and face flushed with excitement.

'But Panduranga! It would endanger my son well being, she said. Panduranga did not reply. Instead he pulled her up and started......

'What you were doing Panduranga, she said wresting herself away from his arms. Shame on you!

But her sleeping gown was torn in the ensuing scuffle and she was without any cover. Panduranga managed to undress his client without any effort. But she was ashamed, more by fear lest

Kaal did not see her naked before Panduranga. He was sleeping in adjacent room.

Kamini had not an iota of doubt that Kaal was peeping through crack of door. But Kaal was enraged. This outrageous scene had made his blood boiling. He would murder this pseudo god ,Kaal had decided. He was about to barge into the drawing room and club him to death.

But the pseudo god had taken avatar of *Kaamdev* to seduce the God fearing lady, blinded by superstition and filial love. The pseudo god had tricked her in arousing her. And managed to undress her. Now she was undressed, covered only with the shame of her modesty and her guilt of being naked before the man other than her husband. It did not matter to her stout sense of modesty and morality that her husband had been unable to keep her happy and give her sons and daughters.

'Devi! You are my goddess; the pseudo god was invoking avatar theory to seduce the devout lady. I am your god. I have taken the avatar of Kaamdev (love and sex god) to satiate the fire of sex that your impotent husband could not. Surrender onto me! Devi! to your Devata. He tried to take her soft and delicate body, with alluring well shaped round breasts carved on narrow waist with broad hips.

'just leave me you brute, Kamini said coming out from his lecherous embrace and giving him a power packed push reeling pseudo god down the sofa. Just go away you leech!

Kala from behind the crack of his room door was boiling with uncontrollable anger. He was about to enter and hammer this pseudo god to death. But then stopped for moment: Why she is doing because Papa is away. Or Papa did not care for her, always trying to be away from her. Why it so? Kala could not make out.

He had not failed to notice that her adopted mother was not happy. He had seen her unhappy and restless, always changing her dress and rushing to balcony and window to stare other men.

Lately Kala had found strange voices of moaning and cooing in strange pain coming out from Kamini bed room. But what was strange that he used to get excited. He proposed to her to allow him sleep in her room. But she had rejected with big no, saying only his dad had that privilege. It had reaily hurt him very much. One night: it was mid night. Kala was unable to sleep. Then he would hear same sound of moaning and cooing coming out from her room. He thought to check just out of curiosity.

He peeped through keyhole. The dim blue night bulb was casting haziness in her bedroom. Nothing was visible at first sight. When he strained, he found her naked gyrating in a rhythm, moaning and cooing with pain or pleasure he could not ascertain. First he felt ashamed of himself peeping into her room. But he could not resist seeing her. He felt like sucking her pink nipple when he was child. Then he got ashamed at such silly thought.

'You are my mother Kaali, Panduranga was saying to Kamini. I am your devotee son..Bless me with you milk.

Now the pseudo god was invoking the universal mother Kaali to seduce her. Oh you are universal mother. Everything comes from you and goes into you. You are only who could give happiness and bliss. Plz allow me to have your milk. You are mother of all beauty. I worship your feet. On Your ankles is resting whole world. Please allow to kiss it. Oh! Your fair and smooth thighs are two pillars holding whole creations. And your sacred vagina is way to your universal womb giving birth to whole world. Let me enter.

He tried to touch it. Kamini hit him with a kick tossing him to ground.

Why not she is calling me, Kaal was pondering. He would have banged this pseudo god head to wall. But for her! He did not like her in skimpy dress that she always used to wear. Much to his embarrassment! Neighbors would find every opportunity to have a look on her. This would anger him so much that he felt like killing them. But for her! One day he asked her not to wear such revealing dresses. But she would burst in anger saying: Now you are trying to have control over me after your dad failed. He could not understand her.

Now Panduranga was trying to use *kaamvaan* (arrow of desire) as last resort. He was invoking the Arjun-Ulapi episode. Devi! It's a grave sin to reject a passionate man or woman. Once when Arjun had gone to Burma, the princess, Ulapi fell in love with him. She was so aroused by the manhood of Arjun that she wanted to surrender to him. But Arjun being married to Draupadi was not accepting her unconditional surrender like you. Then she invoked, God knows what scripture saying it is sin to reject passionate man or woman.

And finally whether God fearing devout lady surrendered to pseudo god or not, Kaal but could not see!

9

Next day: Kaal confronted her mother. He tried to re-enact the pseudo god: Mother! Hungry and thirsty. Please give me your milk......

He was thrashed and shut in the room. Next day his father would arrive on short notice. There would be endless discussion going on. The closed room conversation would be happening most of the time. Kaal would be packed to a boarding school. His mother would join his father in far way corner of the region.

Thence would start the life journey of lone child! A man born with frown! Life, world, people, relationship, society, community-everyone frowned upon him. And he in turn frowned them. Kaal never went back to home. Kaal proved his name-Time and like it kept on moving in life, never looking back.

He never went back to home, even during holidays. He did not feel like going home as it no longer appeared like home. Home is not made of four walls. The relationship, love, mutual bonding and feeling of security are invisible thread weaving into a home and family. One could feel un-homely like even at own home. On the other hand, one can feel home like even in other's house. Or in company of friends, acquaintances, strangers or even amidst visible and invisible enemies one can feel homely. And many have been doing so!

After School, college or university break, he would go to his new universal home: Ma Kaali temple. She was his mother, father, brothers and sisters, uncle aunties. She was his home, family and whole world. He appeared isolated and desolate to others, but he was fulfilled.

After one year of his shifting to hostel, he stopped accepting money from his old parents. As he had started getting scholarship, stipend and honorium from the government agencies, school, various social institution. His academic and non-academic performance were so excellent that he would be honored with scholarship and stipend from Middle school to college to university! And till he would take up the job of an alchemist at one man run lab of the scientist, Yug.

Ma Kaali had become everything for Kaal's life. She was always with her and he used to invoke her presence and company at the drop of hat. The universal mother-Ma Kaali was his everything and by constant remembering her, he would became one with her. And sometimes he would feel like Ma Kaali himself and other time her son, daughter, lover and beloved. He would develop many feminine traits and feelings along with masculine. And over the years Kaal would became an epitome of Ardhnarishvar (half man and woman)

Then Kaal was in the college. It was his Final years of the study. He was living as paying guest of a family. The family was in the line of farm trading. He would do the baby sitting for the baby of the working daughter-in-law of the family.

One day the baby was very hungry. But she would not be taking any feed. Her mother was not breast feeding him for the fear of losing her perfect figure. Even though his pot-bellied husband did not care for figure in woman, she was obsessive about it. For this reason, she would have mothered the test-tube baby.

The baby was crying non-stop. Kaal had tried every motherly thing. But she would go on crying. Then he took her in lap and tried to press against the chest. The baby would stop crying. She was busy taking breast feed from Kaal's chest. Kaal overwhelmed with motherly feeling could not be sure baby was getting milk or not. She was busy shucking his nipples with utmost satisfaction.

Slowly and steadily there came a transformation in Kaal. from being Ardhnariashawar (the half male and female), he became the virtual being of Ma Kaali herself: out to recreate world. He did not tell anybody as they would term him mad. It was matter of feeling and only self could feel it.

'Really! How come, Maan but could not help form interrupting Kaal. He had been listening to his story for long. Then why you are here instead of recasting the world.

'Well…. Kaal fell silent for a moment, taking a long breath and then releasing said. To recreate something already existing, it has to be partly or wholly destroyed. Only then new can be realized.

'Oh I see, said Maan with sarcasm and doubt not with a pinch of salt but all salt instead.

Kaal but could not fail to notice it.

'You know, when one realizes his or real being that is all permeating, all pervading observer Soul encased in body, he or she becomes Soul of all, consequent upon Soul being one, indivisible and universal. He or she feels doing even his or body not doing and work done by other is also his or hers.

Maan thought this man had gone nuts. He is just mad and if I stay any longer with him, I may also go mad. Better quit this bizarre man and place.

He would take leave from Kaal very next day.

2
NEW KINGDOM OF LIFE

Maan again out in the wilderness of bewildering beauty of Lahaul Spiti! Alone, without any purpose, any goal, any motive! No idea what to do, where to go: but zeal for life would be there. Like zealots or new converts, he was bubbling with life. Life it was certainly and he wanted to live. Out in open: with infinite sky overhead and sky rocketing mountains with ice capped tops and panoramic valley.

To live was the life and living itself for Maan. For that matter it seemed for everyone as well! The routes and paths of the life, literally and metaphorically both, were destinations themselves, at least from hindsight. Autumn was silently taking the valley and mountains in its fold. It was noticeable at first sight. Its effect was perceptible with leaves getting yellowish hue and trees foliage thinning out. A change was taking place stretching from outside to the inside and from inside to the outside.

After saying goodbye to Kaal and Tabo, Maan arrived in Sangala valley of Kinnaur by hitchhiking and using available mode of transportation. It would take almost two days to reach there. The high rise mountains with snow laden tops, the river and rivulets flowing down the valley and glaciers upstream glistening in sunlight greeted him with élan. An ecstasy of unknown seemed to be beckoning him! Maan got down from car he had had hired.

Fresh and life giving air would greet Maan in open. With his rucksack bag on back, Maan started walking down the road. At every turn new landscape was unfolding: the same mountains and valley with sky overhead stretching to horizon and beyond but different view. The same life but different scenes and seers and seen, like one on board a boat and feeling the trees and foliage on riverside moving despite being stationary!

Maan was just moonstruck with unfolding beauty of life! No sooner he would behold one scene, another would start unfolding before his eyes. No less mesmerizing and fascinating than other, appearing different and diverse but being one. Just like life with all colors and hues and nuances greeting at every instant and moment. Every moment new vistas opening before the eyes, complete in itself. Comparing, tagging , coloring it with our color seems to be problem, Maan was thinking. Perhaps memory and thoughts not allowing to see them, enjoy them as they are.

Lost in the reveries of previous moments, the succeeding moments and instances are lost at the altar of memory, thoughts and expectation of unknown and un-beckoned. The unfolding beauty of life would be lost at every moment. No sooner one moment, one instance unfolds than shadow of previous and future moments, instance wouldovercast them.

Maan has been losing life, its moments, Instances for the moments and the instances to come. That too would be overshadowed by past moments and instances, memory and thought. Just like he was missing this landscape unfolding at this turn for the next landscape about to come, and its essence not realized as self would be grooving in the preceding landscapes, Maan was thinking.

On the next turn, the river flowing beneath had taken a sharp bend. There appeared big caravan of shepherds, sheep herds, goats and a few yaks. A thin cloud of dust overhung was also moving along with them. The road was blocked. The traffic of one or two vehicle was stuck up. The horns were blowing rather with shrilling effects, even though mixed with the chimes of bells tied in the neck of sheep herds in cankerous harmony.

Pacing up his steps, Maan had overtaken the caravan with a sort of relief.

'Babuji...Babuji.... o jeans wale Babuji..., someone was calling behind. Maan had gone a few yards ahead of the moving caravan.

A beautiful girl in her early 20s, in dusty tribal dress was calling him, while running towards him. He stopped.

'Recognize...you gave 10 Rs in Kaza, she said with sly smile. Taking out the note from her low cut *choli*, she thirst into his hands, thinking he might not take it back.

'what money...when, returning the Tener, Maan said. He was unable to remember.

By then her mother, pretty tribal woman in her late 30s with queen like beauty and manner had arrived.

'Jau Babuji! Ho remember ...in Kaja market, she greeted with mysteriously coquettish smile.

'Oh! Yes you!..Got it, Maan remembered that brief encounter with two stunningly beautiful tribal women. How could he forget the two pairs of blue and brown eyes! They had been haunting him for quite a few days.

'But don't want to take back money, Maan said pushing back the hand of the girl gently.

The girl's mother took out money from her daughter and gently put into his breast pocket.

'where you going sahib, asked the mother.

'Not anywhere..actually just having a look around, replied Maan.

'Then be our guest tonight, she said with putting stress on night.

'Babu!, the girl's father had joined. Just see how do we live. Stay for day.

The father was saddled with small statured horse, paired with other horse that was of her partner's perhaps.

Maan but could not miss the offer. He had nowhere to go and nothing do: a dry leave like, at the beck and call of wandering winds! Allure of nomad life! Shepherds! Cows, sheep, goat and Yak! Krishna, Jesus, Moses life stories!

1

The caravan of shepherds Maan agreed to stay with was not ordinary one. It was big caravan of wandering nomad tribe. It had adopted shepherding as front profession. Behind it was involved in a lot of illegal and illicit activities- liquor supply, manufacturing and trading in *ganja* and *charas, Kesar*, dry fruits trade, tiger skin and bones trade, herbs and herbs based liquor. When the law red flagged its illicit liquor vending, it shifted to herbs based liquor which was not banned.

The caravan had thousand of live stock of cows, sheep, goats, yaks and horses. There were 50 shepherds to tend them. It had 100-strong army to protect the caravan and carry forward its host of legal and illegal activities.

It has its own version of nomad King, queen and princess. There were a set of norms and rules n regulations as evolved during course of its economic and non-economic activities. The father was king, the mother was queen and the girl was princess. Maan had noticed all of them wearing an insignia of pantheon carved on their dress and garland.

The caravan was a sort of nomad tribal kingdom wandering all over the middle and higher Himalayas. It would pitch its camps on strategic places. Generally it was in difficult terrain where no could dare to venture in. It would station on strategically vantage location where demand and supply chains of their various shady trades could be carried out.

They had got modern tents with heating system and all modern facilities. They would have mobile solar panels and equipments to generate electricity from live-stocks dung.

The wandering tribal kingdom had various small units to take care of live-stocks, horses, technical matters, arms and ammunition, general administration, food, various trade units headed by one head person. The overall command rested with tribal king.

But in this tribal kingdom the real king was the queen. Maan came to know about on very first day of his stay. The caravan had pitched tents and camps on narrow gully surrounded by mountains two sides, flanked one side by stream and other by river valley. The tents and camps were established on a plateau fortressed by rocks and boulders jutting out. On rear side livestock had been placed, encircled with camps and tents of shepherds, armed units, various trades and units of kingdom.

Overlooking these camps and tents on inclined ground was the tent palace of Queen bee-queen in king. Seated there with king, queen and princess was Maan, having tea and *kahwaafter* partaking customary tribal wine, weeds and joints of cannabis. They offered tribal wine, herb made wine, but Maan was teetotaler. He preferred cannabis joint that the Baba had offered in Kaaza. And queen been had specially made for him. She also shared the weed with Maan. It was sign of special affection that king had noticed from very start.

'How long you would go with us Babuji, asked the king sipping from his pint of liquor. The caravan had plan of going towards Badrinath, from there to Bharmour, Hadsar and Mini Kailas and beyond.

'O God! You would go that far, said Maan looking towards queen bee. He noticed that she had not approved this rather unfriendly question by her husband. It was akin to asking a guest as to how long he would stay with host.

The queen gave stern look reprimanding him. And the king would change the topic. He started sharing the information regarding shepherding, milk delivery and other trades. Maan hardly understood what he was saying except some familiar or common words as he was talking in nomad language. But he had to listen and show to them he was getting their point. Most of the time queen eyes were on him prying from all angles. And she was doing it openly.

The caravan was resting. Soon it would sleep, even if it was hardly 8 Pm. The arrangement for Maan had been done in a sort of outhouse of Tent palace that was in the farther corner. There were two cutout windows, one opening to stream and other towards valley with river flowing glowingly. Amid such panoramic view Maan was feeling happy and adventurous. More than being happy and adventurous, he was happiness and adventure himself. A sort of strange feeling no words, phrase could describe as it was beyond any word, thoughts and experience.

'Lo Babuji milk.., came queen bee with glass of goat milk. The princess following her: Both were in traditional nomad dress with lot of beads and garlands revealing and concealing the necklines.

Before Maan could ask her to sit down, she had placed herself at the edge of bed. The daughter was standing and sometimes eying Maan and listening to mother talks. She was talking without stop. She would complain about her husband. She would cry at the weak and alcoholic king. She would curse her fate. She would say her husband was no good in any respect.

She told her daughter to go away and sleep. She would start telling how unhappy she was. She had to look after everything. The king of tribe would not do anything but the drinking. She was confiding many things but Maan could not understand. He was just nodding. Then she would start crying.

'Don't cry, Maan was consoling her. Everything would be fine.

But she kept on crying. Then he started patting her all over and kissing. She had almost surrendered to him. Maan did not fail to notice what she desired. Neither she tried to conceal nor expressed overtly. But then her daughter would be calling. She went away saying she would be back within a hour.

The night was starry outside. But stars seemed to have descended in his tent. He could not but feel that the night was singing a song of desire and lust. The desire seemed to have lusted him making his all sense prying for that. The primordial desire for lust appeared the meeting point for modernity and tribal. And Maan was feeling at ease with it.

The queen bee went to king lusting for his share of honey. He was sore with his inability to enjoy honey as drunkenness had pepped up the desire while back up force had depleted. And she knew he would come in his usual tepid way. Now a new bee had come and she would pour honey on him. A bitch would always be bitching, the king knew it well. She had always been sleeping with one or other shepherd or army men. The strong man Gabru had been a consistent lover, king was thinking. Why she was not coming?

He would ask queen to massage or press his body. It was only conjugal bliss he could afford. Drunkenness had rendered him capable only for this carnal pleasure. Even this was being denied, he would get angry and call his daughter to do the needful. The incest and incest relations, starting form tribal have continued even among the moderns. Some tribal moderns have legitimized and legalized these taboo by making it part of social code! The marriages and sexual relations among blood relations have been given strange color of customs and traditions!

For tribal king such things don't merit any consideration for regret or repentance. He knew that she had gone to Gabru to tell that she had found another one to satiate her insatiable lust.

2

The starry and dreamy night would stagger on. Maan felt as if there would be no morning. But he was sure queen bee would come. She had gone to Gabru's tent, a 20 year shepherd man. She had taken him as lover to break his marriage with her daughter. The family had decided to get their daughter married to him. But queen bee did not want. She wanted her daughter to marry one of the powerful nomads. It would increase her power, riches and reputation. She deliberately enticed Gabru and surrendered to him unconditionally. Who would dare to spurn her!

No body, Maan was thinking, could be immune from her dazzling beauty. She would be his one day! This had seeded his whole being ever since he met her for the first time. Since then it had been there in some or other corner of his heart. He had no compunction in accepting to himself that he had come here just for her. And she would come and redeem his feeling.

Maan did not know she had to cross two oceans to reach him. Now she was in neck deep with Gabru. She had gone to inform him she would come to him after mid night. But he had sensed that she would never come. She had found a new lover in Maan. Everybody knew except the new lover. And Gabru wanted to extract as much honey as he could. Afterwards it would not be available.

Then she would have to deal with crib that king had become. When she reached the tent Palace the king was trying to crib with her daughter. There ensued a long battle and fight over this. And it was almost past mid night. But the lamp of hope was burning on both sides.

When she reached Maan's corner, he was past the sleep.

She just switched off the lamp and became one with him. In the darkness: The heart of darkness becoming one with periphery of darkness.

3

The morning after the darkness was like every morning. The Sun would be slowly emerging from beyond the mountains, rivers, trees and the foliage getting crimson hues, in expectation of new beginning. The life would get back to its usual start. Birds, animals and whole animate and inanimate beings would get new things to do and be. The outside would be penetrating with usual dose of illusion and the inside would get pregnant with outside giving birth to inside-outside hyphenated world.

But the morning after meeting of heart of darkness and periphery of darkness was unlike every morning. The morning Maan got up was simply a morning, very unlikely of the morning! There would be no hangovers of previous mornings and their memory. He was not himself but just being and doing. A process of the doing and being, not the doer but floating in floats some like reality!

The caravan had moved on, setting for the mountains of Badrinath. When Maan came out from tent palace, the tents and camps were gone. The livestock had moved on and related paraphernalia disappeared. It was wilderness again. With litters and left outs reminding the life that once was. But living was there.

The queen bee, king and princess were awaiting Maan. A bonfire was burning to wade through the morning chill. They were discussing the matters with their personal footmen as usual. Queen greeted him with zeal of last night. The king ignored and the princess had winked. For servants and footmen it was normal.

The tent palace was unfolded and tucked onto two horses. They would move on their respective horses. The queen had arranged a mere for Maan knowing he would be riding first time. This mere was beloved of her horse so that Maan horse would never stray from hers. They would be always following each other. Within half an hour, they overtook their caravan on the move towards the mountains of Badrinath.

Maan was riding on the horse first time. Galloping on narrow path flanked by towering mountains and deep river valley, Maan felt unknown unfolding on precipice. In beginning a fear seemed to be hung over nowhere but it was there. The fear of unknown was greeting at every step. But soon it would peter out into nothingness.

It had started with riding mare, Laali. First Laali would not accept Maan. She had tried to dismount him. But with queen around and after letting her have some fresh grass from the overland she became friendly. And the ride was smooth in quite contrast to bumpy zigzag path, walking on edger's raze like feeling would be hitting the guts. The steep ascending and descending serpentine paths and gully would give the terror like chill to the heart.

Sometimes it would appear life about to terminate. Next moment would the bend of steep path unfolding beautiful landscapes, making life more precious. How small and insignificant one would feel before these imposing and towering mountains, trees and deep river valley, Maan would think while passing difficult and imposing mountainous terrains.

But if became on with them, one would feel big like them!

Maan but could not help from wondering! Life and death situations would be appearing in tandem, as if the continuation of one life process! At one moment death would be lurking off the precipice of the cliff hanging over thousand feet of abyss. Next one would be overwhelmed with abundance and vastness of life. Amidst the beautiful and fascinating landscape, cascading streams above from mountains tops life would be overflowing with passion and zeal of living and the life!

Life and death would appear, to Maan, more often than not as one. And he would wonder as to why we humans are so afraid of death when it remains like shadow right from birth. The life would seem to be living in the shadow of death but making it as shadow of terror and fear. Maan would feel like having new lease of life.

If death seems to be shadow of life just as our shadow is to us, there appears no reason for us to be afraid of death. If the life ends to get more life or new lives, so does the shadow of death. But Maan would be unable to make out the opposite: death is but shadow of life, it remains all along the life and like our shadow but here life seems to be living in shadow of death, not death as shadow of life.

Laali, the mere had jerked, stopping at the middle of steep ascent. Maan would pull the rein to move her ahead. But she would refuse to move. She was in no mood to budge even an inch. No, not ready to go. Queen bee and princess had galloped ahead of the sharp bend of the river Alkananda and Laali was refusing to move. The king was farther behind, down there in valley, seated on jutted rock and doing his favorite pastime-drinking. Queen bee had been behind princess whose horse had been berserk most of the time. And the princess was having difficulty in reining at her command.

'Somebody might have given wine or drug to her horse, queen bee had said muttering to Maan anxiously. It might be Gabru or …. She went ahead of Maan. Otherwise she was always with and around Maan. She feared some revenge or jealous attack or treachery. It is for this reason that she had arranged Laali, a mere, who was attached to her stud horse!

But the mare Laali would refuse to move. She might be feeling deserted by queen stud horse. Even Maan had started feeling like deserted and a sort of lonely when queen had gone after Princess jerking horse. With the queen gone and the jealous king on his tail, Maan was getting jittery, sweating even in chilly air of high Himalayas. And Laali would be moonstruck of her stud refusing to move! He kicked her, cajoling with stick, but of no avail.

Maan would dismount in dejection. Plucking some mountain grass from behind the rock he offered her. But no, she would not even look at it. Then he started patting her, taking her red and white face in arms, hugging her. Even kissed and implored: Darling! My Darling Laali, chal move please and re-mounted on her. Lo and behold she stated moving, swinging like Nag and Nagin dancer. Immense happiness and sense of relief would come to him.

Happiness, joy, sorrow and life and death, Maan was thinking riding through cliffs hangar mountains and terrain of Badrinath area, appear like fleeting but intrinsically interrelated. One is following other and that too at thought level. Fear also seemed to be having no ground other than on thoughts. For that matter life and death also seems to be following in succession … life and death too … or death stationary shadow of life… That too seemed to be rooted in thought or conditioned or wired with fear of death. Every activity of human life seems to be conditioned with fear of death or death! As if death not life is the moving force of world, life and beings.

..Culture, religion, law, society and even business like insurance, beauty and gym, medicine, Maan was thinking, all appear to be invoking the fear of death to fulfill their respective objective and interest. Even politics and culture seemed to be invoking fear of death in the form of annihilation, destruction and ignominy ... domination and dominated, suppression and suppressed. Death or fear of death seemed to be shadowing the life whereas it appeared to be mere shadow of life! Maan could not help but conclude in rather offbeat way.

The caravan would start moving with outbreak of the morning. When the shadows of evening began falling on the mountainous terrain of high Himalayas, the tent would be pitched. The camps and make shift tent house and palace would be erected. The livestock would be made to be rested. Their routine economic activities would continue. Even while moving the caravan would be doing its activities. The route that caravan would take was off the beat one: short cut but very difficult and arduous and dangerous.

The danger would be there lurking every moment. Steep incline and decline, cliff hanger, trudging on narrow and treacherous path, snow and glacier would be there to be wary of. Then the possible ambush and attack arising out of inter as well as intra tribal rivalry and jealousy, power struggle were there to cope with . But so was opportunity for economic activity and well being. The saffron, *shilajit Kesar*, tiger bones, skin of various animals, cannabis and herb based liquor and weeds!

4

Seven days of steep ascending and steeper descending. Sometimes so steep even the horse had to feel difficulty. They had to ascend with the horses dismounted. That too so with much difficulty, gasping for breath, resting after few steps for sometimes! Only then the caravan had managed to reach Badrinath.

The camps and tents were pitched in other side of Hanuman Chatti with unhindered view of Nar and Narayan Mountains! River Alaknanda cris-crossing between this two grayish blue mountain like the Devi of bliss and happiness! Glacier of Maana, the gateway of Swarg from where five Pandav brothers along with Queen Draupadi and Kunti had entered the Swarg, joining each other beyond the fascinating bend of Aleksandra!

When Maan first saw the Gateway of Swarg or Heaven, he felt as if this gateway or *dwar* is heaven itself! This moment, this instance seeing the fascinating scene-Glacier of Maana with its white cover of snow bathed in high altitude Sun, joining the river beautiful Alaknanda and sentinel like bluish mountains rising higher and higher and merging with infinite sparkling blue sky! A surreal fragrant wind blowing and transcending the being to unknown and nothingness without any worldly limitation! The mind going beyond the joy and happiness, self beyond trials and travails of life, ups and downs, sorrow and happiness, beyond binaries of life: one with all and All in One.

It would appear as *Swarg* or heaven or ultimate aim or logical destination of life itself! Maan would feel like having attained *Swarg* or heaven or Kingdom of God! It appeared as if he had attained the liberation, had lived the life in general and this is life in particular. Even if death comes, it would be not death but life itself.

No less living the life was the route and period that would sally forth Maan along with his caravan to this heaven on earth. This moment, this instance stretching and including the sum total of all preceding and succeeding moments and instances. Two points but looking one instance and moment joined by the invisible dots. Life and death, happiness and sorrow and other binaries appearing but manifestation and continuation of this one instance, one moment stretching to all and stretching back to one!

The precipice of stuck up and stuck up in precipice! Cliff hangers! Hanging valley and rocks! Valley of flowers! Narrow river valley getting narrower, steeped mountains getting steeper, accelerating ascents meeting the decelerating descents!

The mornings in the caravan would break out like all mornings: new hopes, new things and eagerness for unknown. For Maan it was beckoning of unknown, but for others it would be the routine. The memory and experience of past would made their mornings as routine. But Maan was like new born; everything would be just new for him. He would regret why he had not lived like now: taking everything, every moment and instance new, as standalone entities, not judged or viewed with other thought and memory and experience. He would often think if it could be done, life would be unabated making of the living as joyful and wonderful!

By the time caravan reached the region of Badrinath, many developments had taken place. The most significant ones was that Mann becoming the king of the Queen caravan. Her old king had fallen sick. She had made him retire gracefully at a village of shepherds. Gabru had been given additional works of collection of *shilajitKesar* and toxic herbs. Now he was no longer seen fooling around her.

The queen would keep the new king always around her. It was a sort of matriarchal tribal kingdom. But there was no gender feeling. It was as natural as nature around. There were no defined relationship and pre-set rules and regulations. Everything used to evolve as per exigencies. It was certainly not tribal or modern. It appeared going beyond these two brackets. A sort of bracket free of brackets!

Maan did not fail to notice that rules and regulations of tribal kingdom were made as per the works to be done or events unfolding. There were no pre-set dos and don'ts but fair play or natural justice was there to guide these activities and unforeseen scenarios. Maan would observe these ideals being followed naturally. These were perceptible in the small activities as well as in big one of the crowning of new king.

There was no fixed rule that such and such or his or her son would be king. Maan elevation as King was decided by the exigencies of time, place and interplay of natural forces. As to queen taking princess future groom as lover was not immoral and unnatural, even though on face value it might appear so. But it was not.

Gabru was only shepherd, marrying her daughter to him would not have fetched any material or greater advantage. Apart from it, having such a stud like Gabru as her son-in-law would have added to the marital discord. And possibility of incest would have always been lurking round the corner in the mobile tent palace!

Gabru would have been crowned new king but for the arrival of Maan. The love or lust angle as decisive factor in the succession of king or leader has been there right from the tribal age. It has survived even now and continues to exist even in the modern times. Apart from dynastic succession, even in the democracy it seems to have mutated into majority favoring one or other dispensation.

The queen was in search of new king for the last few years. Seeing the failure of the old king on all fronts, she had started exploring the possibility of finding his replacement. When she had seen Maan loitering out in Kaza and evincing keen interest in her, she had enacted the drama of Rs 10. She had enough money but to attract the intervention of Maan she would create the scene.

After taking over the charge of new kingdom, Maan had made positive interventions in its state of affairs. He would tick off some economic activities of the kingdom, red flagging the liquor, tiger hunting and trading in cannabis and related substance. There were protests from many quarters. Even queen would make long faces when the proposals were put before her. She was the de facto king, reigning the kingdom with all her charm and ruthlessness.

It rather would prove to be very arduous proposition to convince her. After many sessions of formal and informal interaction, even on bed, she conceded to relinquishing some activities. But on tiger hunting, she was very adamant. It was very lucrative business for them. The tiger skin and its bones, particularly its penis was in great demand among the Chinese and Mongolian tribes.

She was not even willing to listen about it. Even if Maan had suggested some alternative source of income such as collecting tax and tolls on various shepherds' routes controlled by kingdom, export of honey and herbs to other countries on large scale. But on matter of stopping the tiger hunting, queen would get angry like tigress. One night when she was mounting like tigress, Maan brought forth this topic very smartly.

'Honey you are powerful like tiger, said Maan after marathon session with her. She was resting on her back. Her tiger skin skirt and choli on her naked body presenting tiger like hue. Her brown hair half covering her tiger like cool awesome blue eyes.

She did not say anything. But in a flash of moment she would jump like tigress over Maan. And another marathon session would follow. She would start clawing, pawing like a wild and violent tigress. Moving like tigress in bed she would start mauling Maan with passion and moaning.

'Darling you are tigress no doubt….but I'm not tiger… remember, said Maan after she had last of her multiple orgasm. She would give a charming, sly smile. He would feel like giving her a long staggered orgasm.

Maan thought it was right time to take up the matter of banning the tiger hunting. He had given her long multiple orgasms. She was resting like satisfied tigress on mountain top! She would never have ever such orgasm even if Gabru, her old king and other lover joined in the act together!

But when Maan tried to engage her on this matter, she would roar like great Himalayan tigress:

'we are going for tiger hunting tomorrow evening, she said roaring like angry and hurt tigress.

It had come like order and final decision. In her own style! Turning her naked back and supine hips towards him, she would go for the deep sleep.

'Tiger the bitch, Maan muttered putting his thigh over her hips in doggie style. But the sleep would not come to him like her.

3
HUNTER HUNTED

Queen did not know Maan belonged to powerful Kshatriya (Ruling) family of ancient India. The fighting, art of wrestling, one to one fight or with multiple was in his blood. Just as horse riding or swimming was! You give him arrow, javelin or sword or gun or A K 47, he would operate like professional. He had not taken any training. It was in his blood: destiny or design or choice, he did not know. But it was there in him!

His family used to have some or other type of modern guns, apart from *lathi*, sword and javelin for self defense. He had used some of the weapons as part of play and adventure. He would still remember! He was a kid, around 8 or 9 year old! He along with his sibling had sneaked the double barrel gun of Papa. He used to take it on hunting. They would try to run the double barrel gun in their sprawling courtyard, resting on the pillar of their *baramada*, to avoid the hard jerk. Even then they had fallen flat after triggering the gun. But they did it!

Maan did not tell Queen he would go for hunting along with his father. Then hunting was not banned. Once when he was child! He requested Papa to take him along on hunting sports. But Maa did not permit and Papa had to follow her order. So his name would be ticked off from the hunting mission. But he would sneak in his open jeep when Papa was going on hunting mission. Once when they were hunting wild pig, a cub was accidently killed. Ever since then he would develop aversion for such cruel sports.

Thanks God! Hunting has been banned and tiger hunting is now punishable offense.

But in this part of world tiger hunting was like old gold rush in Africa-the heart of darkens. There was mad, frantic and often bloody rush for tiger hunting. There would ensue big gun fights, raining of poisoned and fire arrows. And more often than not all members of some or other tribe would be wiped out of the life. Many tribes had been ruined in this mad and bloody war of tiger hunting. But few had risen powerful and dominant by controlling this tiger hunting turf. Tiger skin, bones and skull were source of immense riches, fetching more value than gold and platinum.

The tiger hunting was source and strategic strength of inter-tribal domination and power struggle! The dominance and power of the tribes would flourish or flounder on this turf. It was for this reason Queen and her tribes' men were strongly opposed to Maan's proposal of leaving the tiger hunting. Maan had provided its alternative.

He had suggested controlling the shepherd's route, ancient trade routes and pastureland, cannabis land and herbs plants area. The toll charged for their use by others could result into no less power and riches than the tiger hunting. But they would not listen. They were unable to understand it. Or old habit, tradition and convention are steadfast in giving to new one, Maan unable to understand.

But Maan had not failed to understand Queen decision of going for tiger hunting that evening. That too on short notice! Even her army and warriors were surprised at her move. But she was the de facto king and king maker. Who could defy or question her! Queen was uncrowned king and ruthless fighter! It was her writ that would be reigning there. Even whole tribal world knew it.

Queen's tribal kingdom was the oldest and richest of world. Once it had been the most powerful tribe, ruling over half of the world. It had civilizational depth and culture like that Bharat from where Maan had come. But it was marginalized due to lack of unity among its tribesmen and branches. It was plundered, and made vassal of two proselytizing tribes.

When these two new proselytizing tribes would be making sword and guns, queen tribe was preaching non-violence, peace and inter-tribal bonding. It was due to myopic, weak and selfish rulers like the old dethroned king that had led to its decline and exile from its own land. It was forced to exit from their kingdom spread over half of Himalayas. It was somewhere between Kashmir and Tibet and beyond in China as Queen had been revealing to Maan during and after their sexual escapades.

She had told how their people would be made bondage by these two proselytizing tribes-Maaru and Chiru. Maaru had entered the scene, invited by one of the warring castes of her own tribe to help one against other. Later on they would become ruler of half of the kingdom. They had converted them to their own religion.

Queen had told Maaru's religion was very primordial in nature guided by the herd instinct. But ironically they would consider themselves as modern. They would be following the middle age practices even in the modern age! They were still under the sway of customs and social practices of incest, marriage relations within close relations and their male used to have six to eight wives. They would kidnap other tribe's women and convert to their religion. They would spread over quarter of world by force, loot and plunder.

The other Chiru, as queen told, were not less ruthless. Chiru would first set their feet in garb of trade. When Chiru saw Queen tribe fighting among themselves, they established rule though divide and rule, using one branch or caste against other. They had also plundered and looted the riches and cultural artifacts of her civilization kingdom. Kaaru would convert her tribe's men and women through force, allurement and by dipping in holy water.

Chiru would first drive Maaru, Queen was telling, out of her land. But by then Maan had converted half of her men and women to their fold. They had also taken away substantial land. Chiru would also repeat same ordeal, though in a bit sophisticated manner. On the loot and riches of Queen tribe, they would become powerful. Both would divide the loot and land among themselves forcing her tribe to be a nomad tribe.

'Since then we have been wandering, Queen had said with tears and despondency in her eyes. Uprooted from our land, without our riches and resources.. We are dwindling tribe and one day we would be no longer remaining on earth ….

'No that would ever happen, said Maan with resolve to restore their glory and land to them. What is situation now?

'Chiru and Maaru has joined together and formed a tribal world organization, Queen informed with helplessness. Through it they are still ruling over the world.

1

Not Much water had flown down the all rivers of Himalayas. Ever since Maan made queen wandering tribe to settle in an sprawling enclave in the Badrinath region. The enclave was surrounded and fortressed two sides by mighty and towering Nar and Narayan mountains and rest two sides by the river Alaknanda taking sharp bend.

It was natural fortress. They could launch their attack from here, but none would be able to attack them. A virtual deterrent like Nuclear or other lethal weapons! It was a sort microcosm of natural city state, built within two years, using rocks and boulders and some light and modern building materials. . Permanent settlements were erected. Palaces and modern buildings were built.

"Now what, asked resting on king size bed in her palace overlooking the majestically meandering Alaknand at the sharp bend. I am feeling like resting and settling for good.

'There is no rest and settling down for good in life, Maan was getting a bit pontifical. The moment you feel like resting, unrest would come. You want to settle for good, life will unsettle for good.

'What do you mean, asked Quinine with alertness of wild cat sniffing some danger.

'Now you have built a natural fortress and your kingdom is secured. This is right time to reclaim your glory, your land and people, Maan was saying, providing her roadmap for wounded kingdom. First bring your lost tribes and people, settle them, and build a powerful Army. Then start making forays into your historical enemies.

'How, not getting how it will be possible, Quinine was confused.

"First you take control of their main source of income and riches- tiger hunting and trade routes. Either you take control of tiger hunting or enforce total ban of tiger hunting. It would ruin their fiancés and they would come at you level.

'But there would be violence and war.., she was doubtful

'Don't you think violence and war is going on even now… avoiding violence or postponing violence is also a violence. Your tribe have been facing violence and war for last hundred years… your land, people, riches, civilizational and cultural artifacts have been taken by them…you have been reduced to wandering nomad tribe…is not it violence, asked Maan looking straight into her blue lake like eyes.

Queen could not say anything.

'if you avoid violence, more violence will follow, Maan continued. It is a sort of vicious circle. The more you will try to wriggle out of it, more it would snare you in its tentacles. The fate of your tribe is there to see it.

Maan would stop for a moment, and then continue: 'After bringing your enemies at your level by ruining their Finances, you establish a parallel tribal world body to theirs. It would reduce their power while enhancing yours… and rest would be decided as and when it is undertaken. The law of karma and series of unfolding events and circumstances will provide you further roadmap… as these are in future, it could not be visualized now. And….

'Leave it my king… I am going to find new young queen for you, said she hugging her passionately.

'you mean you are going to find young king for you… go ahead.. but spare me…love, peace, pleasure are but escapism, signature of escapism… not facing reality…. Maan was disgusted.

He would take her leave saying he was going for horse ride to Swarg Dwar or Gateway to Heaven.

Queen knew he would not return. Good riddance! She fell flat on bed, dreaming about new young king!

PART
4

1
WORLD WAR OR PANDEMIC

Maan would hit out the roads to the wilderness again. This time, wilderness of urban metropolitan chaos! But how strange it was! Instead of chaos, chaotic silences would be quivering with doomsday aura there.

Over there, here and everywhere! Not a single person seen as if humans had deserted the planet and gone to some other planet. Or war had been declared! Or Kala would have started his mission to change the world, Maan was wondering!

It was seemingly pandemic time. A horrendous pandemic appeared to have taken world in its sweep. Everything-airways, railways and roadways had been shut. People were locked down in their homes, a total lockdown in force. Roads, squares, malls, shops and market places were shut. Global village would have been shrinking to the isolated homes.

A war like situation! A scenario of war without having the war declared! Third world war appeared to have been fought and won over. Invisible and unacknowledged as war!

Third world war indeed had been fought and won by Kina, a Kamnist rogue state. But Maan did not know then. He could see the collaterals of war there and everywhere! Locked humans in the confine of homes, terror struck, gasping for relief from overcast shadows of death. Everything would appear to have been destroyed. The world had been surreptitiously and smartly attacked by bio-weapon of deadly virus, stored in its lab.

One night Kina army had overtaken the lab silently. They would let loose the bio-weapon on world. All worlds appeared to have been defeated. But this defeat would be termed by the defeated powers of the world as pandemic. Just to fool people and hide their defeat and cowardice, world leaders and powers appeared to have termed it as a natural calamity and pandemic. Or Kina was able to manage them to see it as such, it depends which way and from whose side it is seen!

It was quiet, deceptive, treacherous and barbaric war. Silently, treacherously fought and won. The adversary and proponents would be both considering it as pandemic. The aggressor had through its proxy world body had managed in its propaganda as not war. But war certainly it was, fought and won by single nation and single deadly bio-weapon. Whole world was living in war like situation. Struck with terror of this invisible enemy! Hiding in their homes for their life and future!

This war! A class apart from other preceding and succeeding wars ever fought in the human history! Its toll on humans, culture and civilization would be far exceeding that of cumulative loss of all wars waged and likely to be waged by humans in the history. Yet ironically it would not be considered war by the victor and vanquished. The world had been Pearl Harbored. With thousand folds casualty, wreckage of economy, people living in terror.

The terror struck humans! Having seen millions dying! Death would be staring at them every moment! And they were dying thousands death every moment. The loss of cash and kinds were immeasurable! The powers that be seemed to like powers that were!

Licking the aggressor, justifying as pandemic!

A natural eventuality! Indeed! But Nature never plays dice! It is human that seemed to be playing a cruel and inhuman dice! Not by human, but inhuman! A Kamnist nation! Kina! Bio weapon! Single nation! Single weapon! All is flat.

Even the gods that moderns have replaced with God were unable to save them. Forget the securing and saving the faithful, the sons and daughter of god, they had shut down themselves. They seemed to be as helpless as humans: the new and effete gods of ideology, technology, consumerism, Swarg, kingdom of god, Jannat and Jihad, proselytizing cultures and numerous bubble some euphoric gods!

"Hey! You! Stop, a Policeman accosted Maan, after trailing him for 10 kilometers of lonely, haunted and barren urban landscape.

Maan was shunted in a nearby hotel: a makeshift quarantine center for being the possible suspects of the pandemic.

1

It was pandemic time. Out there in Karat and whole world! A vanquished world order! Everything in life had vanished! Undeclared war- Third World War! Fought and won! Invisible bio-weapon! Invisible war but visible collateral loss of War! Gargantuan and mindboggling collaterals and effects! Moderns seemed to be living a primitive life! Xenophobic and claustrophobic life style! Back to primitive life and life style! Amidst the crumbling silhouettes of modern culture and civilization!

But for the rest of teeming billions of world! It was pandemic time!

Kaal was stuck up in a hotel at Manali. Along with an American tourist, an African student, and A Thai wandering man! Microcosm of world! Or world itself seemed to have been locked down! Like animals in cage! A seemingly eternity of uncertainty would be hung on their face and beings! Covered in pall of gloom, invisible veneer death and fear of death would be lurking round the corner!

Kaal's partner was stuck up thousand miles apart in Mumbai. In hotel she was holed up, all alone with herself and her unrequited dreams and fantasies. She had gone for seminar, and seminar had ended well before the nationwide lockdown was announced. But she would overstay? Why? She wanted to relish being alone and at large with her secret desires running wild. To find wings?

Kaal had wanted her to come along in Manali, to chill out together. He had planned to pep up their sagging marriage life! But instead she thought to do it alone by going to attend seminar. Kaal was wondering, is she alone or with someone? He was holed up here with three foreigners she was suspecting his multiple partners!

'Oh! I see, she had mocked with disbelief and suspicion. For foursome quarantine!

Kaal could not listen further. He had hung up.

Holed in dormitory, all four would seem an isolated islands floating on the edge of life and death!! They would appear to be having drifted to their respective continents! Despite staying put in big room!

The American tourist in quarantine with Maan would remain lost in the reveries of his holidays in Los Angles during last Christmas. He had opted to stay here. He felt more secure here than his country where thousands had died and more were dying daily! But his hearts and mind would still there. His family there and he had decided not to go back. How helpless and disgusted he must be feeling, Kaal was thinking.

There out in open! Millions of migrant workers would be stranded along the highways, roads, streets and lanes and by lanes. . Desperate to meet their family out in villages and countryside! They would be walking under the scorching sun to go to the safety in peace of their villages.The inhumanely treatment of their plights in the urban jungle was more heart wringing than that of pandemic that had rendered them insecure and terror stricken.

To be one with nature- all inclusive rural bondage, they would be risking life! They would bear the vagaries of nature, callousness of fellow human beings, and dirty politics of the politicians. They would be bearing all these just for the love of their family, security of community and peace of countryside.

'O bhai! Never come again this heartless place…said, Guddu Ram, a migrant worker stuck up in another state while on his way to his native place, to his leader, Ram Jatan . He was commander of 20 laborers hailing from bordering districts of UP and Bihar.

'Hundred per cent right *kahehain*, said Ram Laal, fellow laborer of Guydu. U netwa told no ration card no food. Made false promise of bus to take us to our *deshwa…sasurkenaati*

'*Ae bhai!* very bad, said another labor with melancholy of a helpless. *No kahana no pina*, not even roof over.

'*Sala netwa* told,you get salary, said other labor with anger. , no need of paying rent..Land lordwa ejected us and *maalikawa* kicked us out from job.

'You are right Bhai!, said all the trapped labors in chorus. We will never come here again. *Apandeshwa* is far better.

A family of four of Sugiya, a native of desert land of Karat, was trudging along the desolate and desolate highway. They were going to their village to feel secured like baby feels in mother's lap . On foot and that too under the scorching sun ! With her frail husband, rendered cripple due to excess work and measly sum in salary. Two malnourished children to look after also! One would be riding the frail shoulders of his father, Bidan Mal. Other toddler would trying to find mother's milk, but it gone dry as the mother had not been getting proper food for last two days of continuous walking.

Media and TV channels were interviewing Sugia and her family. Rich and powerful were taking selfie with her family offering food. But she and family would remain hungry. Yet they would keep on walking on foot to go their village, 500 kilometer away.

One night her husband would die in mid way. Next day toddler would pass away. Now people were flocking in doves to help her. But the surviving child was the problem. Had she been alone, she would have got all help. But she did not stop. She would keep on moving on. Even though she had hardly covered 20 km of 500 km

But the Time would not seem to be passing for Kaal. The Time itself would appear to be holed up with him and other fellow foreigners in the quarantine center. Even the time was looking like as if got infected with virus. This is what a terrorist and jihad do: create terror and fear in the mind of the people. Make their life hell with fear and terror from visible and invisible, perceived and non-perceived enemies. And finally they would listen to them, concede to their narrow and sectarian demands!

'o shit man! The African student shrieked. My smart phone has been infected. It's not working.

Everybody looked at him. But nobody would utter a world. Then everybody would lapse back to their respective cells of isolation and islands of desolation.

'It's not pandemic, Kaal tried to bring back the drifting continents back to the center, conversation. It seems to be bio attack.

'Agreed, says Thai wander wonder. He had been wandering all over the world. But now holed up here!

'I don't know, African student chuckled. My study has gone blink. Career is bleeping red.

The American tourist nodded in affirmation. But did not say or add anything.

Then there was silence again. The gurgling sound of river flowing aside Nature's Trail park, chirps of birds, Bulbul singing, even a Robin humming in nearby Jungle of Devdars and pine trees would start filling up the silence.

The American tourist would look through window the mountains surrounding the Rohatang pass. He was missing Rocky Mountains. The African student would be lost in the dream of the Pilipino girl he had met in Manali. They had decided to go Malana and have joint there together sitting on cliff hanger banks of Parvati River. But for this pandemic!

Kaal was thinking about his partner. He was terribly missing her and the family life. And her partner, thousand km away in Mumbai hotel, was sitting near window, watching deserted Marin Drive. Life seemed to have deserted everywhere and her too. She had thought she would freak out in and around Marine Drive and Chaupati. But this lockdown! Pandemic and......

Kaal's partner was alone in the hotel room. How many days she did not want to remember! And how long she would not care to think! She had stopped thinking about the days to come or anything in future. She often would get more anxious and lonely when thinking about future. When future in itself uncertain and yet to unfold itself, thinking about in such abnormal time like this had become a sort of taboo for her. She was trying to live moment by moment.

Whatever every moment would bring out for her she was accepting with a sort of equanimity. Without any if or but or any regret for this or that happening or not happening. There was no other option available either. The mobile phone was only her companion. And the television and radio her room-mate to fall upon when everything would seem to be ripping apart! She would talk to Kaal and the friends and the office colleagues. But even that seemed to have become a routine.

But she was getting bored, being all alone in the world reduced to her hotel room. She would be sleeping and pacing inside her room when tired of everything! When these would fail to sooth her fragile being, she would step up in the corridor of the hotel, pacing up to and fro. Even that option had been limited, as some portion of hotel had been turned into quarantine center. As the cases had been growing exponential day by day, the hotel management had issue strict order to the resident of hotel for staying put in their respective rooms.

Neha, her cousin had rung up yesterday. She was getting scared even living with family as the paying guest in Bangalore. She was doing her second year of MBA. There was end semester exam to be held and she had prepared reading day and night. But now exams had been postponed, colleges shut and the exams cancelled due to nationwide lockdown!

Now what! Neha would wonder often while shut in her room. When she got bored, she would come to the drawing room. She would watch TV along with the uncle and auntie and had some formal talks and conversation. But the uncle and auntie would always be busy talking to their son over phone or Skype. He was stranded in US. He had gone there to pursue higher study but could not get admission in any college. He was about to return, but for this worldwide lockdown.

Lately Neha had started having fits of dread. Life was going to end and she had not seen the world. She had a number of things to do. She wanted to go abroad and have the feel of the great life there. Till yesterday everything was going well. And then this pandemic and lock down. She was wondering why they would call it Kovid 19 and why not krona. Sometimes they would call it this and some time that. While earlier they used to call it Kinese virus! What was happening!

Moderns have developed strange kind of ways. They usually do not mean what they say and not say what they mean. This syllogism of hiding behind phrase and phraseology seems to be endemic. But if one goes deep into it, its nothing but standard response to every problem. To hide behind fabricated truth, the truth and knowledge already cancelled.

Sometimes she would feel angry and frustrated with life and world. And all the people who mattered in this regard would become the cause of her ire. Why not they are doing anything to Kinese! They must be punished; their bio-weapon factory should be closed down. And they must compensate for such loss and suffering. Everyone is suffering, even animals seemed to be disillusioned. Uncle's dog seemed to be always lost somewhere and most of times listless. Auntie cat had become more shy and fearful. But some would say this not bio-weapon, a natural calamity! Natural My foot, muttered Neha trying to control her anger.

'Its not natural, Kaal was discussing with his co-partners in a makeshift quarantine center in Manali. Nature never plays dice.

'There you are buddy, the American tourist was coming out from his self-enforced isolation and desolation.

'krona virus has been there, but never so deadly. It has been certainly tweaked with, Kaal said.

'Some scientist says it might have mutated, added the wandering Thai guy.

'That does not seem to have any credence as virus never have been found to mutate laterally. It is manmade. It is a sort of Frankstenian monster that after devouring its maker out to devour whole world. it is deliberate….malicious use…a sort of hidden war, Kinese krona devilry, Kaal would say frankly.

'You are right. Kinese lied people died, the American tourist said. They hid the fact from world. When confronted, they said we had brought Krona virus. Its nothing but projection of their malicious act.

He stopped for a moment, then said, I tell you they gonna pay heavy price for it.

Then all of them would lapse back in the confounding

silence, all of sudden. Some invisible enemies seemed to be lurking in the half dark and half lighted room. Kaal felt the shadow of death lengthening and overshadowing all. What a great way of nature or existence to realize the fragility of life! It is lived in misnomer, Maan was thinking. The misnomer and folly that he or she is body only and it is dying every moment or living every moment to die. But it is realized only in crisis or death like situation.

Even Kaal would remember the real nature of self only when such life threatening situation would arise. Is it existence grand plan to make us realize our real self and nature of our being by throwing us in situation, Kaal was pondering over. Or refusal to realize its true nature invites such dread and discord in life, he was unable to decide.

2

Sugia, family of migrant worker, only surviving child had also fallen ill. She was put into a roadside quarantine center with her. There had come a break in her homeward journey. But she was feeling this also as journey to her home village. The people would be helpful providing all possible help. She was rather overwhelmed. Death of Bidan Mal, her husband had rattled her. But he was dying even before the actual death. He was suffering from tuberculosis.

After the death of her family members, everyone had become good with her overnight. They would became very good mannered and large hearted. Death had such sobering effect she would not have imagined. Does it bring goodness in people or people do it out fear of their own death invoked by having seen other dying. And this krona! Is it illness or some invisible enemy out to gobble up all. She had heard about plague that had struck her great grandfather's time. But this illness was killing people more fastly than scythe cutting the grass!

That afternoon Kaal's partner was in the dread of life. She was not afraid of death. She feared she could not live a life she wanted. She could not do what she had been cherishing for long time! She felt as if life would be slipping from her grasp and she wanting to cling it! Claw it! Paw it! Wresting what could be grabbed from the moments and instants from the life holed in fear and terror!

Then her whole being would start rebelling against her. She found within her a rebellion brewing up. Then it would engulf her, stretching beyond herself, her life and whole creation. She was meant to enjoy, she was woman and her being asking for to be loved and loving. Why she should feel any constraint when she was free. Lying on the bed she would feel her love life had remained unrequited and life going to end. Kaal must be enjoying there with foreigners. He had said he was with males but she suspected the all females. A flood of jealousy and revenge had been overflowing her since then.

There was knocking at the door.

'Room service, it was room service boy.

'Come, she replied lying on her bed. She was in all see through lingerie, further shrinking upward showing her all vitals. She did not feel like changing the dress or straighten the lingerie. Let him see, she thought and got a warm hook in her heart travelling down below, stretching her legs wide apart!

The room service boy came hesitatingly.

'Go ahead, she said. I am damn tired, she stretched her body.

He started doing room service.

'Do you have any massage service, she said getting a bit nervous. Her heart was pumping like it would come out in open.

'No madam, its closed, he said staring her almost naked body.

'Do you know some body who could massage.

'No, he said. His eyes remained glued to the revealed vitals.

'You know how to massage, she asked.

'No mam..'

'Oh then I would teach you. Come along, she said pulling him down to her.

Neha was wondering how her sis- Kaal's partner would have been coping up the lock down. For her it was like one day passing like a year. She would try everything to pass the time. But it was being very difficult. She would feel being caged like animals. And the caged passion was trying to find its escape. She had noticed uncle would be leering at her. Whenever auntie was not around, he would take some or other sort of advances.

One night he had gone too far in his madness. He came to her room just to ask how she was doing! And then he started lot of things she did not like. When she wanted to excuse her, he offered a sort of lollipop of her being suitable bride of her son. And he would try to do what the prospective bridegroom would not have thought it fit to do. She got very upset. She requested him just to leave her alone. Otherwise she would call auntie. And he did go away out of her room but had placed himself outside her half opened door. And he would start masturbating fantasizing her, ensuring it that she would notice it.

Strange and disgusting! What a horrible time to live in! And such horrible act, Neha but could not help feel the madness and abnormality having creped every being. And the time and place would lose its boundary.

In makeshift quarantine centre, Kaal too was bored. He would feel jaded to the hilt. He but could not help feeling anguished and enraged over this whole of affairs. War like situation but not considered war. Living in terror and dance of death and destruction all round, but it is pandemic and natural calamity!

African boy was only happening being! Always busy, listening to music or humming some popular tune he would be. Only happening thing!   Dancing and clapping! Sometimes he would break out into solo African folk dance. How much similarity it has with Santhal and Kol of our country, Kaal would often wonder.

Every life matters but why it is so that black life has to assert that theirs life also matter. This is the tribal fault lines perhaps, running under current in the moderns-race, color, caste, language, kinship, and tribal like religions: instead of liberating and giving happiness, dividing in us vs them like hostile and divisive binaries! Every protagonist would like the world crowded with their own religion and culture. They would be doing all sort of inhuman and cruel acts in name of religion and culture. But they would call it a piety, civilizing the uncivilized and the jinxed brotherhood and fatherhood!

Kaal would remember the assertions of many French and English intellectuals. The world was living in harmony with gods and humans sharing common importance on equal footing and as one. It must have been epitome of Brahma- All is one and one is all! Society and community was living in peace and harmony. Conflicts would be managed in friendly and humanly manner. But with arrival of two modern proselytizing religions and cultures! Everything would be hierarchical , inclusive, us vs them, higher and lower, the difference and exclusiveness would be norm. All sorts of exclusive and primitive identity and norms would be presented in the overtones of modernity and inclusiveness.

But how would these bleak days pass! It had become only issue with them. When nothing to do, the idle mind would become centre of all types of fear and morbidity. Kaal was always engrossed in thinking about his partner. It had become rather favorite time pass. But recently he found a strange internal transformation gripping his being. He would start thinking as if his partner were thinking. What would have she thought if she would have been locked down with three males! She would have fantasized about this and that. By constantly being in her shoes, he came to know that she must be having flings with some or other person.

A transformational sort of things would overtake Kaal. He seemed to be exiting his self and entering that of her partner. His self seemed to be replacing itself and taking over hers. The pleasure and pain, the fantasies and quibbling of woman like her partner would become as if he were she. He could not understand this change taking over his being. Has he gone nuts or some sort of insanity is happening to him, Kaal often would think. Is it some sort of coping strategy to wade through abnormal time? Or some sort of abnormality or anomaly? Is it sign of homosexuality taking over him indirectly?

Otherwise Kaal would not have felt like what Kajri-his partner was feeling at subtle and gross level. Kaal was just at loss to understand why Kaal ceding himself to his partner at all level. It might be unconscious projection of his suppressed or unfulfilled sexuality finding some satisfaction in that of Kajri having nice time being all alone and free to do or be as per her fancy! He that has become she at ideational level was having marathon fling with African boy. Then American tourist and then Thai wander man and on and on....

3

Nature never plays dice (Einstein). Based as it is on infinite series of cause and effect, how could there be a chance or dice like dicey game! The cause of a substance or phenomenon leads to effect, and the effect becomes cause of the effect of next series, and on and on. It has been going since time memorial and beyond, and will continue to be so infinitely and indefinitely in time. It is human or nurture that decodes chance factor to subserve its subjectivity: sees what it wants or unable to see!

Primordial being seeds it own being. And that being becomes the being of the world. One substance becomes Purush (Pure Consciousness) and Prakriti (nature).In cause and effect conundrum like chicken egg syndrome One Substance causes the effect of Purush and Prakriti: one is invisible but lighting all making things exist, observing all, making all to be seen, permeating and pervading all like primordial being.

Other is visible what is world or Nature or nurture. At subtle level (practical, day to day life) a substance or phenomenon becomes so when we see it or consciousness (Chetana) become conscious of it. Otherwise a matter is not matter, a table is not table unless we make it.

Likewise Kaal seems to have seeded Kajari: a female being

seeded by male, another's being   in his being. There should not have been any problem, ideally speaking, as it seems to be replication of creator and creations process. But for the ego (ahankaar) of Kaal,it would prove to be problematic. To seek pleasure, to move the time staggering and halting, to make up for the infidelity of his partner and avenge it perhaps that becoming the effect of the cause. But the ego (*ahanakar*)that he is doing seems to have become the problem and occasion of conflict.

It is not coincidence that it is ego (*ahanakar*) of Primordial Being that has led to creation of life and world. That is what Krishn has interpreted the creation of world! When Uddhav, Krishn cousin, asks him why world has been created, Krishna says that it is because the Primordial being or Super Soul or *Paramatma* wanting to play (do Leela) the life by becoming the life, living and world Himself (Herself or gender neutral or beyond it)!

Kaal would invoke the subtlety of woman though Kajari, his partner. He would try to pass the abnormal time having befallen before him. The limitation of time, place and circumstances becoming the incubation ground for all sort of beings and free play of instincts and desires!

... She is bitching.... he that has become she at ideational level could also do the bitching..With one and all, as per fancy! The matter of morality and sinning comes when one is caught by other or own self... do it secretly without knowing... knowledge has been cancelled, morality and God has been replaced with a number of fallacious demi-gods and gods.

.. After all we are modern... nothing matters more than multiplicity of being and its feel..LGBTQ if it empowers..to wade through abnormal time...to plod the unprecedented situation and circumstances... that is what life seems to be like..One has just to be for being in itself…

There has been no problem ever since! For Kaal, except that whenever he thought he is the doer and enjoyer. The problem of existence becoming nightmarish prospect would crop only when he would think himself as doer and enjoyer. If he would not think about it, he would be existing with ease and enjoyment! And that is what he has been doing, not thinking. He thinks, therefore he does not seem to be existing! But when he does not think he seems to be exiting! Perhaps!

Thus has been the problem of existence and existent! A process that existence is, life is! It is ours loss if we consider it as fixed entity or judge able and justifiable being. What could be conclusion of a process that keeps on going, renewing and recreating. The process that life is, would be riding on unending series of cause and effect or *Karmas*.

And the end, summing up and conviction and judgment would be faltering on infinity of finite beings being woven on perennially on cause and effect or Karmas. In nature or in universe, it is cause leading to effect and the effect becoming cause for further effect. It is on and on…..

LIFE CHURNING.....

Maan was baffled! He would not believe it is the same world! And the same life he has been living through! A complete change has factored the world. Its social and political order has changed beyond recognition. The Third world war or pandemic has transformed the world beyond any imagination. He could not believe it is the same world order he has been existing in!

Man has been transformed from a social animal to that of social distancing and isolated one. Desolation and solitude has become new social matrix. The mutual suspicion and otherness bordering on negligence and a sort of hatred has come to the fore in stark contrast to earlier when these tribal instincts were dormant. Not acknowledged at face value even if doing the same. The Old normal has become abnormal and abnormality of isolation and desolation new normal.

The centre of power has shifted. The periphery has become the centre and the centre still grooved in the centrism despite the loss of power. Human history has been hinging on tribal credo of violence and war. Every strand, every stride has been following and preceding this primeval credo of violence and war, even though smartly disguised in respectable jargon and phrases. But the undeclared war and its declared colossus collaterals seemed to be having unhinged the world for time being.

Maan but could feel the fear of invisible enemy, the dread of unknown lurking at every corner and doorsteps. The squares were deserted. Boulevards were without colors. The joints and hubs were bristling with wary and isolated people. Love and relationship were floundering on fear and suspicion. Fear of invisible and unknown seemed to have become new god like that of tribal and primates.

The history of humans seems to have come back to the square! From where they have started from tribal or pre-modern age! At least at existential level

Maan would be unable to decide about his life and the world. But what had happened or would be happening seemed to be what life is all about. It would appear to him never ending process, keep on going even if death, destruction and desolation seemed a temporary aberration apparently! Life would keep on churning new beings, new life and world. It is continuation of that process: existence becoming existent and existent melting into existence to become existent again!